JAZZ and PALM WINE

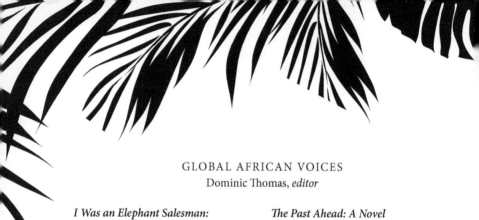

GLOBAL AFRICAN VOICES
Dominic Thomas, *editor*

I Was an Elephant Salesman:
Adventures between Dakar, Paris,
and Milan
Pap Khouma
Edited by Oreste Pivetta
Translated by Rebecca Hopkins
Introduction by Graziella Parati

Little Mother: A Novel
Cristina Ali Farah
Translated by Giovanna Bellesia-
Contuzzi and Victoria Offredi Poletto
Introduction by Alessandra Di Maio

Life and a Half: A Novel
Sony Labou Tansi
Translated by Alison Dundy
Introduction by Dominic Thomas

Transit: A Novel
Abdourahman A. Waberi
Translated by David Ball and
Nicole Ball

Cruel City: A Novel
Mongo Beti
Translated by Pim Higginson

Blue White Red: A Novel
Alain Mabanckou
Translated by Alison Dundy
Foreword by Dominic Thomas

The Past Ahead: A Novel
Gilbert Gatore
Translated by Marjolijn de Jager

Queen of Flowers and Pearls: A Novel
Gabriella Ghermandi
Translated by Giovanna Bellesia-
Contuzzi and Victoria Offredi Poletto

The Shameful State: A Novel
Sony Labou Tansi
Translated by Dominic Thomas
Foreword by Alain Mabanckou

Kaveena
Boubacar Boris Diop
Translated by Bhakti Shringarpure
and Sara C. Hanaburgh
Foreword by Ayo A. Coly

Murambi, The Book of Bones
Boubacar Boris Diop
Translated by Fiona Mc Laughlin

The Heart of the Leopard Children
Wilfried N'Sondé
Translated by Karen Lindo
Foreword by Dominic Thomas

Harvest of Skulls
Abdourahman A. Waberi
Translated by Dominic Thomas

JAZZ and PALM WINE

EMMANUEL DONGALA

Translated and with a foreword by **DOMINIC THOMAS**

INDIANA UNIVERSITY PRESS

Bloomington & Indianapolis

This book is a publication of

Indiana University Press
Office of Scholarly Publishing
Herman B Wells Library 350
1320 East 10th Street
Bloomington, Indiana 47405 USA

iupress.indiana.edu

The paper used in this publication meets the minimum requirements of the American National Standard for Information Sciences—Permanence of Paper for Printed Library Materials, ANSI Z39.48–1992.

Manufactured in the United States of America

Cataloging information is available from the Library of Congress.
ISBN 978-0-253-02669-9 (paperback)
ISBN 978-0-253-02675-0 (ebook)

1 2 3 4 5 22 21 20 19 18 17

CONTENTS

FOREWORD

Harmony and Liberty or Jazz and Palm Wine

EMMANUEL DONGALA was born in 1941 in the Congo (Brazzaville), a former French colony that achieved independence in 1960. That historic moment coincided with Dongala's decision to study in the United States as one of the first African recipients of a Ford Foundation scholarship. This decision, which would ultimately shape both his professional and his literary trajectories, was very unusual at the time given that the vast majority of francophone sub-Saharan high-school graduates able to pursue advanced studies abroad would traditionally travel to France. Dongala spent time in New York perfecting English, and then studied at Oberlin College and Rutgers University, returning to the Congo in the late 1960s. Shortly thereafter he left once again to complete his doctoral training as a chemist in Strasbourg, France, only permanently settling back in the Congo as a professor at the University Marien Ngouabi in Brazzaville in the 1970s.

The Congo's political history has proved to be a turbulent one, and the country has been witness to multiple coups d'états and coup attempts following independence on August 16, 1960. Fulbert Youlou served as the first president and was followed shortly thereafter by Alphonse Massamba-Debat (1963–68), who implemented a scientific socialist line. He was replaced by Marien Ngouabi in 1968, who proclaimed a People's Republic only to be assassinated in 1977. Joachim

Yhombi-Opango was then appointed to head an interim government. With the exception of a transition period between 1992 and 1997 that included a national conference and during which time the country held its first democratic elections (the office of the presidency was held by Pascal Lissouba), Denis Sassou-Nguesso has been the country's unchallenged dictator (1979–92 and 1997 to date).[1]

During the civil conflict in the late 1990s, Dongala and his family were able to leave the Congo and move to the United States.[2] This was made possible through high-level diplomatic intervention by the U.S. State Department; a number of U.S. intellectuals and politicians with whom Dongala had established friendships and relations over the years also mobilized immigration efforts. He was offered a professorship at Simon's Rock College of Bard in Great Barrington, Massachusetts, which was also hosting the great Nigerian writer Chinua Achebe (1930–2013). As Dongala stated in an interview with *New York Times* journalist Michael T. Kaufman in 1998, the civil war "was more horrible than I could have imagined as a novelist"; having said this, he was eager to underscore how he had suffered not "because [he] was a writer or an intellectual" but rather "like everybody did because the mortars and the rockets we call Stalin's organs kept firing on our house, because anarchy spread and children with machine guns took what they wanted. It was not ideological."[3] However, Achebe, the acclaimed author of the masterpiece *Things Fall Apart* (1958), immediately identified the plight of the fellow author whose own international reputation preceded him.[4] Achebe stated that "Neither of us had to leave. I came after my accident, and then things back home became so much worse. Now every letter I get from home tells of ordinary people suffering, disappearing, being killed."[5] This complex and entangled history has shaped the man, the scholar, and the writer, and Dongala has acknowledged that "because of the time I had spent in America, I developed a certain way of seeing things, a certain concept of freedom, a way of saying what one thought, of reading."[6] This fascinating life journey, which has seen him crisscross the Atlantic for almost sixty years, lies at the heart of *Jazz and Palm Wine*.

The great Martinican poet Aimé Césaire famously writes in *Notebook of a Return to the Native Land* (1939) that "my mouth shall be the mouth of those calamities that have no mouth, my voice the freedom of those who break down in the prison holes of despair."[7] While perhaps not fully embracing his esteemed predecessor's position, and writing in 1979 that "I am not a spokesman for the 'people,' I am no one's messenger," Dongala nevertheless enjoys status as one of Africa's most important writers and as someone whose writings have relentlessly featured ordinary people, concentrated on the tenuous relationship between the individual and the collective, and explored the struggle to achieve forms of peaceful coexistence.[8] In the process, he delivers piercing critiques of political authority, making extensive recourse to humor and irony, exposing the contradictions and hypocrisy of postcolonial leaders, subjecting these corrupt rulers to greater scrutiny, and ultimately compelling readers to rethink the contours of civil society. This occurs first in his novel *Un fusil dans la main, un poème dans la poche* (1974; A gun in the hand and a poem in the pocket), in which Dongala turned his attention to the hopes and aspirations of the anticolonial struggle and the subsequent broken dreams associated with the failure and disillusionment of political independence. Later works, *Le Feu des origines* (1987; *The Fire of Origins*) and *Les petits garçons naissent aussi des étoiles* (1998; *Little Boys Come from the Stars*), reckon with the challenges of narrating history and establishing shared memory in the face of the distortions associated with dictatorial monolithic rule; *Johnny chien méchant* (2002; *Johnny Mad Dog*) addresses African child soldiers, and more recently he considers the social condition of African women in *Photo de groupe au bord du fleuve* (2010; Group photo on the banks of the river).[9]

Many if not all of these questions are explored in *Jazz and Palm Wine*, first published in France in 1982. Although the actual stories included in this collection were written at different historical moments, compelling links are evident between the two parts, namely "an African one and one that takes place in the United States. On the one hand 'jazz,' and on the other 'palm wine' that symbolizes an African facade for me."[10] As critic Séwanou Dabla has written in addressing the historical interconnectedness, "from symbol to symbol," Dongala throws "a bridge over the Atlantic [. . .] reconciling two peoples separated by history."[11] The first part is consciously and deliberately anchored in postcolonial Congo, where the book was censored until 1992, and it features protagonists who, having overcome decades of colonial exploitation, now find themselves wrestling in their daily lives with a burdensome bureaucracy, oppressive legal system, and corrupt nomenklatura.

In "The Astonishing and Dialectical Downfall of Comrade Kali Tchikati," a former party leader who has fallen out of political favor now finds himself—much like the central protagonist in "Old Likibi's Trial" who is struggling to end a devastating drought—caught in a conflict between customary beliefs, which are often founded on a belief in animate nature, and the scientific and rational explanations expected by the newly installed secular scientific-Socialist or Marxist-Leninist governments.[12] Likewise, "A Day in the Life of Augustine Amaya" features a poor market trader wrestling with the reasoning of an oppressive state bureaucracy, and in "The Ceremony" a young militant endeavors to make heads or tails of the official party's rhetoric in order to improve his own social standing. Citizens of this rapidly mutating postcolonial society thus attempt to meet their daily subsistence needs in the face of a self-serving rapacious elite with an insatiable appetite for power, and in a context in which paranoid leaders are themselves entwined in a circular logic that calls for vigilant monitoring and repression mechanisms that underscore their own vulnerability and fear of being overthrown, as the story "The Man" powerfully demonstrates.

The last two stories of the collection prove to be equally unsettling as the author navigates the unrest characteristic of the context of the civil rights movement and violent repression of civil rights activists in the United States during the turbulent 1960s. This was a time that witnessed the assassination of John F. Kennedy in 1963, Malcolm X in 1965, and Martin Luther King Jr. in 1968. The autobiographical story "A Love Supreme" highlights the genuine inspiration Dongala found in John Coltrane's music, while simultaneously offering insights into Dongala's own understanding of art: "During the '60s, I watched the closest companions of my generation sacrificed, massacred for the beliefs they held: believe me, J.C., your music upheld their faith. That's the artist's triumph over political militants, neither trying to persuade nor to bring happiness, at times even against their will; the artist allows each individual the pleasure of self-discovery as well as the discovery of those marvelous and extraordinary things that must exist somewhere out there in the universe . . ."

For Dongala, the pathway to harmony and the key to individual liberty are to be found in artistic expression and creativity. In fact, the interconnectedness between the multiple spheres exemplified by Africa, America, and African America are contained in the story that bears the title of the collection itself, "Jazz and Palm Wine," strategically located at the intersection of the African and American spaces, in which Dongala adopts a universal framework, bringing together world leaders as they confront a common threat presented by invading extraterrestrials and who accomplish reconciliation thanks to jazz performances while consuming vast quantities of palm wine: "All of a sudden, from everywhere around, the houses, the inside of the Earth, from Space, the enchanting sounds of John Coltrane's saxophone reverberated. And the creatures started bobbing their heads, their eyes seemingly frozen. It wasn't long before hundreds of square miles of land were transformed into a mass of heaving bodies transfixed by a possession-trance dance rhythm."

As Dongala has argued, "What I think is so tragic is that almost nowhere in Africa is there a civil society outside politics," which means that "it is so easy for people, even writers, to be corrupted by politicians," whereas "writers should be against the powerful."[13] The stories in *Jazz and Palm Wine* are thus of tremendous pertinence to contemporary conversations on identity, race, and coexistence, providing contextualization and a historical dimension that is often sorely lacking. Writers have a key role to play in reminding leaders that they are being watched, that the citizens they are supposed to represent expect transparency and good governance and will hold them accountable for their actions. These thoughts are echoed in the words of contemporary African authors Alain Mabanckou and Abdourahman Waberi, for whom "the life span of a dictator can be measured by the magnitude of our silence."[14]

Dominic Thomas

Notes

1. For a more detailed overview of this history, see John F. Clark, "Congo: Transition and the Struggle to Consolidate," in John F. Clark and David E. Gardinier, eds., *Political Reform in Francophone Africa* (Boulder, CO: Westview Press, 1997), 62–85, and Dominic Thomas, *Nation-Building, Propaganda, and Literature in Francophone Africa* (Bloomington: Indiana University Press, 2002).

2. See Julie Michaels, "Writer in Exile," *Boston Globe Magazine*, February 6, 2000, 12–31, and "African Novelist and Chemist Emmanuel Dongala," interview by Terry Gross, *Fresh Air*, http://www.npr.org/templates/story/story.php?story Id=1121385, April 12, 2001.

3. Michael T. Kaufman, "Arts Abroad: Reflections on African War, from a Haven in the U.S.," *New York Times*, May 7, 1998.

4. Emmanuel Dongala has received numerous literary awards, including the Prix Ladislas-Dormandi, Prix Charles Oulmont, Grand Prix Littéraire de l'Afrique Noire, Prix RFI-Témoin du Monde, Prix Fonlon-Nichols de l'excellence littéraire, Prix Virilio, Prix Ahmadou Kourouma, Prix Cezam, and the Prix Mokanda.

5. Chinua Achebe quoted in Kaufman, "Arts Abroad."

6. Interview with the author, Brazzaville (Republic of the Congo), December 21 and 22, 1994.

7. Aimé Césaire, *Notebook of a Return to the Native Land*, translated by Annette Smith and Clayton Eshleman (Middletown, CT: Wesleyan University Press, 2001 [1939]), 13.

8. Emmanuel Dongala, "Littérature et société: Ce que je crois," *Peuples noirs, Peuples africains*, no. 9 (May–June 1979): 63.

9. Emmanuel Dongala, *Un fusil dans la main, un poème dans la poche* (Paris: Albin Michel, 1974), *Le Feu des origines* (Paris: Albin Michel, 1987), *The Fire of Origins*, translated by Lilian Corti and Yuval Taylor (Chicago: Lawrence Press, 2000), *Les petits garçons naissent aussi des étoiles* (Le Serpent à Plumes, 1998), *Little Boys Come from the Stars*, translated by Joël Réjouis and Val Vinokurov (New York: Farrar, Straus and Giroux, 2001), *Johnny, chien méchant* (Paris: Le Serpent à Plumes, 2002), *Johnny Mad Dog*, translated by Maria Louise Ascher (New York: Picador, 2005), and *Photo de groupe au bord du fleuve* (Arles: Actes Sud, 2010).

10. Interview with the author.

11. Séwanou Dabla, *Jazz et vin de palme de Emmanuel Boundzéki Dongala* (Paris: Fernand Nathan, 1986), 56.

12. Throughout, the influence of Kongo culture is tangible. For exhaustive studies of Kongo religious cosmology and political culture, see Wyatt MacGaffey, *Modern Kongo Prophets: Religion in a Plural Society* (Bloomington: Indiana University Press, 1983), and *Kongo Political Culture: The Conceptual Challenge of the Particular* (Bloomington: Indiana University Press, 2000), and Simon Bockie, *Death and the Invisible Powers: The World of Kongo Belief* (Bloomington: Indiana University Press, 1993).

13. Kaufman, "Arts Abroad."

14. Joan Tilouine, "Entretien croisé avec les écrivains Alain Mabanckou et Abdourahman Waberi," *Le Monde*, May 23, 2016.

JAZZ and PALM WINE

The Astonishing and Dialectical Downfall of Comrade Kali Tchikati

The day will not save them
And we own the night.

LeRoi Jones (Imamu Baraka)

One of the things I really like doing when I arrive in a new place is to venture out late in the day, at those inchoate and fugitive hours when the daylight begins to fade and darkness gradually spreads its cloak. Those early evening hours give you a good indication of a city's secret pulse, of its hopes and fears, a glimpse of all that still hesitates to appear or disappear, a moment when people and things were the most off-guard. This is also the time for new smells, when the wood-burning fires or kerosene lamps were lit, when hurricane lanterns and candles suddenly appeared, flickering just like a thousand fireflies in the night sky, all carefully lined up along the sidewalks where vendors sold manioc, skewers of meat and grilled peanuts. . . . And then there was all the hubbub, sounds unique to each city, composed of stifled voices, the cries of mothers beckoning their offspring to return home, barking dogs, loud engines, and all the local nightspots bellowing out the latest tunes. Lovers could be spotted on the street corners relishing the anonymity afforded them by the vanishing daylight, the first ladies of the night loitering close by, nocturnal butterflies transformed into obelisks and rendered strangely desirable by the soft velvet of the moonlight. These intervals in time were inebriating, hinting at the proximity of those forces that filled the African nights!

The city I found myself in on that particular night had something more to it though: the distinct murmur of the ocean and a light salty breeze. Just as in port cities the world over, with the cosmopolitan fauna of foreign sailors waiting patiently for nightfall in order to disembark, leave their comfortable element behind for a few hours and enjoy the pleasures on dry land. There were also lots of Cubans around, the rear guard following those who had already landed and made their way to the battlefields in neighboring Angola.

So I strolled along the streets of Pointe-Noire with the pleasure that comes from being on terra incognita, especially when, as was the case here, there were no street names or numbers. Directions were given out in such a way that you had to find your bearings in relation to various landmarks, such as a shop or a well-known watering hole. I continued to wander aimlessly and, by the time I'd reached the Ntiétié neighborhood, had been engulfed by the night. That's when I started searching, unsuccessfully, for a taxi so I could make my way over to the Widow Djembo, a restaurant and dance bar some friends back in Kinshasa had recommended. Tired as I was, I decided to grab a beer across the street at a bar called Josepha, quench my thirst and take in some of the local fraternal warmth in this popular hangout.

No sooner than I'd sat down than some big guy, and I don't quite know how else to say it, basically marched in like some force of the night wearing a long colorful boubou, with a bushy beard and thick disheveled hair, and a talisman around his neck like the ones the Senegalese marabouts sell. He seemed totally disoriented, like a lost seaman, a drifting vessel in search of the safe haven of a port in this somewhat chic bar. A peculiar combination of power and desperate solitude emanated from him. But what was all the more peculiar was the fact that there was something familiar about him, and the more I observed him, the more I became convinced that I knew him. He didn't sit down but instead went straight to the bar, as if he wanted to quickly throw one back and then head back into the night from which he'd emerged and continue on his journey. I searched my most distant memory, recalled images of acquaintances that even vaguely resembled him, but still didn't come up with anything. I eventually just sat back and savored my own drink.

* * *

Folks in Pointe-Noire have the reputation for being heavy drinkers, of both beer and imported red wine, which means that at this time of the evening they swarm the local watering holes like nocturnal insects drawn to the light, looking to assuage a great thirst accumulated throughout the day in this city that, despite its proximity to the ocean, is always particularly warm. Folks are generally in good spirits, charming and fun to be around, even if, in the same way as people who hail from the south, like I do, they're ultimately vain, more often than not boastful, yet, and this is a somewhat likeable characteristic, also especially fond of women. So there I was deep in my sociological ramblings when I felt a friendly tap on my right shoulder followed by an exclamation of surprise.

"Well if it isn't Kuvezo!"

"Oh, it's you!," was about all I could come up with as I desperately worked my gray cells into action because he at least had recognized me; his name . . . was right there on the tip of my tongue . . . I almost had it . . . fiat lux, and then suddenly, like a lightning bolt: "Kali Tchikati! It's you, Kali Tchikati, I can't believe it, what on earth are you doing in this place?"

"I should be asking you that, dear old Kuku. . ."

"You're still calling me by that ridiculous nickname. Here, grab a seat. What's the latest? Tell me! What are you drinking, my shout."

I didn't have to ask him twice, but he really did seem happy to see me again. Believe or not, it had been a good five years since our last meeting, right around the time he'd been expelled from our one-party government that controlled everything, every gesture and every thought. He ordered a large bottle of red wine as any local son worthy of the name would have done; we continued our exchange of pleasantries until they brought over the bottle.

"Let's drink to our health and our reunion my dear Kali," I said, raising my glass.

"And let's not forget our ancestors," he added, pouring a few drops of wine on the ground.

At first I thought he was merely continuing to mock those theoreticians of the myth of authenticity he'd spent much of his life, as a good progressive, railing against. And yet there was something about this gesture of his, how should I put it, something genuine, almost an act of faith. It actually caught me off guard, but I didn't think about it for long. And so we drank away, me with my beer and him with his wine, that awful red wine the French sent our way when they cleared out their cellars and vats, one glass of which was enough to trigger a stabbing migraine that would last for hours. The wine didn't seem to affect him in the same way, although after his first glass the initial enthusiasm he'd shown when he first spotted me had worn off entirely and was now replaced by a worried look. Something was clearly plaguing him. But what could it be?

"Tell me Kali, what's bothering you? You look worried, as if the demons of the night are after you."

"That couldn't be closer to the truth! I am being hunted."

"By what? By whom? I thought your problems with the party were behind you."

He didn't say anything for a while, then downed half his glass in one gulp and continued.

"My dear Kuvezo, you have before you someone who is about to die. I've been bewitched by my paternal uncle."

Those were the words Kali hurled at me. For a second there I thought he was kidding; in fact, I almost burst into laughter and was about to tell him that I wasn't that gullible, but then thought better of it when I saw the desperation in his eyes, big open windows into his deeply troubled soul. I could see this was serious. Nevertheless, I still had difficulty believing his sudden "conversion," in getting my head around the fact that Kali Tchikati of all people could possibly believe in witchcraft or at the very least in the kind of mystical or metaphysical beliefs which our people held on to so dearly. I couldn't help probing a little further.

"You, Kali, bewitched? You're pulling my leg, right?"

"There's no doubt about it, my uncle wants to 'eat' me."

"Come on now, really, you the steadfast materialist, with six years of ideological training in Moscow under your belt, the former direc-

tor of the party's school and head of ideological propaganda, you who
wanted to convert all the temples and churches into museums, you. . ."

"I get it that this must be hard for you to believe."

"You bet!"

He didn't respond, just took a few more swigs of red. I also kept
quiet, feeling a bit guilty, that I'd perhaps been overly harsh with a
friend who clearly needed to confide in someone who would listen
to him. That said, I was really struggling to come to terms with this
new Kali Tchikati sitting opposite me. I could still see myself argu-
ing with the Kali of old, my friend-adversary with whom discussions
had always been frank, and often also quite heated, violent even. We'd
fallen out on numerous occasions but always made up again. He was a
childhood friend, and we'd been at middle school together at the Lycée
Savorgnan de Brazza. I also knew his father, who'd treated me like his
own son. When we graduated, I went to America to study the physical
sciences while Kali headed to Moscow to study the social sciences, in
the aftermath of the popular revolts that swept away the former re-
gime. We both returned to the Congo at about the same time, give or
take a few months; I became a professor and disappeared into relative
obscurity at the university, while he quickly rose through the ranks,
becoming an eminent member of the newly established party, second
in command in the hierarchy right after the head of state who served
as its president, because he was at once the director of the school and
the head of ideological propaganda, in other words the guru of the
future red leaders that the country would train. Six years in Moscow
was no small feat! And that same guy was now sitting right in front of
me, talking about witchcraft and curses with even greater conviction
than I'd ever had, me who had always taken safe refuge in that gray
area in which one couldn't really separate belief from disbelief, much
in the same way as most people are aware of the limits of their own
knowledge. Kali had been of those who, in his hour glory, had been
responsible for the atmosphere of intellectual terrorism in the country,
claiming they knew best what the "correct political line" for the Revolution should be, falsifying history, stifling a wider public debate of
ideas under a form of centralism that had nothing remotely democratic
about it, censoring writers and artists, imprisoning journalists. And

I won't even mention the way they treated political opponents. It just didn't make any sense . . .

And, as always when one doesn't quite grasp something, silence takes the place of words—which is exactly what I resorted to—right after ordering another beer. Fate had already played its part bringing us together again, the loud music and crowded bar a haven of sorts, such that even if someone had wanted to eavesdrop on our conversation they wouldn't have been able to. A few prostitutes were looking our way determinedly, beckoning us into the night. Perhaps contrary to our good morals, these girls at least had peace of soul. This thought brought me back to Kali, who also seemed to be relishing the silence of the night in this questionable place in which we could barely hear each other.

"Kali, why don't you tell me exactly what went wrong and what's going on now. Tell me the whole story, don't leave anything out, I'm your friend."

"You don't need to ask, you know, Kuvezo, I'd already decided I was going to tell you everything the moment I spotted you. I now realize that you're the only friend with whom I've always been able to speak frankly. So, let's start with my wedding . . ."

" . . . at which I was one of the witnesses."

"That's right, you haven't forgotten, have you?"

* * *

"I'd just come back to the Congo after years of studying abroad and wanted to marry a girl I'd met in Moscow, a fellow compatriot; a nice-looking girl, from a good family, and smart as a whip who'd just gotten her doctorate in sociology. But there was, how should I put it, a 'blemish' on her résumé since we weren't from the same ethnic group. You understand the scandal I caused when my paternal uncle summoned me to let me know he was opposed to this union. I went against their wishes and challenged them on the basis of my ideological convictions. You remember the exchanges, right? 'You're our son and we don't want anything bad to happen to you; but just as true as it is that we are your fathers, the words we pronounce today will be realized and this in spite of your education and all those fancy diplomas you picked up in the white man's country'—a few drops of palm wine poured on the ground out of respect for the ancestors, a few drops drunk and spat out for the wind to carry wherever you decide to go—'we're telling you: you will not be able to have children, your wife will not procreate, we don't want any offspring from the belly of this outsider'—more wine spat out, a knot tied into a piece of red cloth, a few more incantations—'we don't mean you any harm, and rest assured nothing will happen to you except for the fact that the offspring of this woman will not enter our bloodline . . .'

"I just laughed at all these beliefs, superstitions. So I just got up and to hell with the lot of them. As long as my wife was in good physical, physiological, and gynecological health, and she was, I saw no reason why the simple words of a bunch of backward illiterates whose reasoning had not even attained pre-Marxist levels, were going to prevent me from having a kid. In fact, I soon forgot about the incident, all the more so because I was consumed with the task of establishing the new avant-garde Marxist-Leninist party in which I was going to be the head of ideological propaganda and the director of the school.

"But then, now married for over two years, I still had no children. My wife was getting more and more worried because she really wanted a child; she was twenty-six years old and could feel herself getting older, and I don't have to tell you the prestige bestowed on wife-mothers in Africa, or rather the stigma attached to women who can't bear children. In spite of her Bolshevik training, she didn't share in my Marxist-Leninist convictions and was starting to seriously believe that my family had cursed us. Initially, she sought salvation in the Christian faith, the opium of the people, and which we'd abandoned over a decade ago. Funny isn't it how people, at times of 'stress,' fall back almost instinctively on childhood superstitions! But for once, Marxism and the Church were on the same page when it came to fighting animist and fetishist beliefs. The Church asked her to stop believing in this nonsense and rather have faith in God the Merciful, and to pray. She even went on voyages to Lourdes and Fatima. But all was in vain since six months later she still wasn't pregnant, and the clergy had been unable to help. She also tried her luck with Allah with the help of a Malian ivory trafficker. That's when she really started pressuring me to arrange a meeting with my family to seek forgiveness through repentance. Infuriated, I decided to take matters into my own hands, scientifically. I arranged for appointments with the top gynecological specialists available; they all reached the same conclusion, that there wasn't anything gynecological preventing my wife from conceiving. Taking advantage of my position in the party, I made up an excuse to justify an official mission abroad, and the two of us set off for France, where she consulted with five different doctors who found nothing wrong with her. And what if I was the one with the problem? And so I went to see five different doctors who found nothing wrong with me, either. But I still wasn't satisfied. And so, as soon as I got home, I fabricated another urgent mission, this time to Berlin, and we both went through another round of tests. And still, they couldn't find anything that, scientifically, prevented my wife from conceiving. By now she was on the verge of depression. Concerned, I made another appointment to see one of the specialists I'd already been to see, explained the whole situation to him, begged him to run some more tests, and to check whether maybe over there somewhere in my gonads or gonadotrophic hormones—I don't know what you call those things, that's not my area of expertise—to check whether there might not be something going on down there . . . and, at my insistence, he did in fact end up finding a little something. After testing my sperm, he found the cause of the problem: I had lazy spermatozoids. Can you believe it! It took them so long to swim toward the fallopian tube that by the time they reached it, they were either already dead or too exhausted to be of any use; or, tired of waiting, the egg had already died. I literally rejoiced, was overjoyed to finally have a scientific, rational explanation. There was nothing mysterious about the fact that my wife had not been able to conceive, it was just that the egg had not been fertilized. Admittedly, only one of the ten or so specialists we'd consulted had detected the laziness of my spermatozoids, and only then following a second visit and because I'd insisted he find an explanation whatever the cost. This failure to reproduce the same results of course went against the principles of good science, but this didn't bother me in the least, I was just so relieved to have found a rational explanation.

"My wife, however, would hear nothing of it.

"'Well, I thought I'd heard it all before. But lazy sperm, well that's a new one!'

"'But I swear they were able to prove it scientifically in a leading laboratory in Germany. My spermatozoids only swim at let's say a few miles per hour instead of a hundred or so, so that by the time they reach their destination the egg has already dried out.'

"'Kali, please, let's get serious and forget about these whimsical explanations and go and see your uncle and paternal family, they're the ones preventing us from having children.'

"Our conversations always ended in that way, over and over again, five, ten times a day. She became more and more depressed and things took a turn for the worse the day after her thirtieth birthday. Our relationship had really deteriorated and so, in the hope of saving my marriage, I decided to make a concession to my wife and to carry out her wish, not because I agreed with her, but rather because I secretly hoped I would be proved right when, having obtained repentance and the family's blessing she still wouldn't be pregnant, my spermatozoids still not going along faster than Jesse Owens.

"I felt so bad waiting for the meeting that I stopped seeing my friends, even you. I asked if the family would agree to meet in my village, far from the capital. I wanted to avoid at all costs anyone from the party finding out I'd taken part in an obscurantist ceremony. And so, the uncles, aunts, and so on were all gathered and then, as was the custom, there was plenty of palm wine, kola nuts, and all the rest. My wife and I had bought five high-quality super wax loincloths made in Holland that had cost 20,000 CFA francs a piece, two demijohns of red wine from Portugal, and a few other odds and ends. I surprised myself, and this was only to make my wife happy—I just started speaking.

"'Uncles, aunts, family members, father, mother, we have decided to come and see you after thinking about this for some time. We are here, my wife and I, to ask for your forgiveness. I have lived with this woman for five years now, I don't want to leave her and I don't want her to leave me. That's why we brought these small gifts for you as a way of letting you know we recognize your authority; we ask for your forgiveness, for your acceptance and for your blessing.'

"My wife was sitting to the side on a woven mat, looking wise and docile. The family elders withdrew and consulted in private. When they came back a few minutes later my uncle, as was customary, announced their decision.

"'Son, we have listened to you, our hearts have listened to you. We didn't want this woman at first, but since she has always shown us respect, since she has never had a bad word to say about us and, finally, since she has come to kneel before us, we accept these gifts. And because you have also come to recognize that one must not disregard the wishes of the elders, we want to let you know that your words touched our hearts. The dispute between us is over. You have our blessing. Go ahead and have children, give birth to boys, girls, twins—palm wine, kola nuts chewed and spat out, untie the knot in the red cloth—there is no longer a problem, you may go in peace.'

"The following month my wife was pregnant.

"Of course, I couldn't make heads or tails of the entire matter. I told myself that it was pure chance, that one of the spermatozoids must have beaten the others in the race. Fine, but then why had it waited five years and the ceremony for it to happen? Of course, it's in chance's nature to be unpredictable, but still!

"We had a daughter; then, two years later we had twins, a boy and a girl. And so it was that after that ceremony, my spermatozoids had definitively stopped being lazy."

* * *

Kali had spoken nonstop, without interruption; he hadn't touched his bad wine during this whole time and only now did he pause and take a sip. Fearing he was going to stop talking completely, I pressed ahead with more questions.

"So, was that when you were expelled from the party?"

"No, no, that was later, but that was when my absolute faith in scientific explanations as well as the unshakeable foundation of my materialist ideology first started to waver. Of course this really bothered me, and as a way of countering this growing doubt, as the party's head of ideological propaganda, I doubled my resolve. So that was when I launched my violent anti-religious and anti-fetishist campaign, the one that caused quite a kerfuffle . . . or so much harm according to some."

Yes, indeed, I did remember two events in particular from that time that had touched me personally, both of which were attributable to Kali Tchikati's actions. The first occurred during a big meeting to support the campaign in South Africa for the release of Nelson Mandela. Midway through his valiant attack on the bastion of Boer imperialist power, Kali was interrupted when the bells from the little church nearby pealed, summoning their flock; he went ballistic. "Comrades," he'd shouted, "these people are mocking us! During a meeting of such great importance, these fools who mislead the people have decided to ring their bells and to try and lure away the people listening to us. This is nothing short of provocation! Just let them carry on in this way and they'll soon find out who's in charge around here! We'll shut down their churches, their temples, and their mosques and turn them into storage space for smoked fish or cement. And in any case, if God did exist, he'd probably be a capitalist, no, worse even, a feudalist . . ." The next day, the party adopted a new measure throughout the national territory regulating the opening hours of churches and times for prayer.

The other incident had been even more strange. A member of the party's Central Committee and his family wanted to build a permanent structure, as was customary in our country, a tomb for a loved one who'd died almost two years earlier. However, the practice was that the tomb be erected during the year in which the person died. Moreover, when they arrived at the burial site, the grave itself was no longer there and no one could remember its precise location. The deceased family member, as one family elder explained, was angry that he'd not been taken care of at the appropriate time and had made the grave vanish. Someone was sent over to the undertaker's office to try and ascertain the precise burial spot, but no one was able to help. And so they did as they would have done back in their village. They gathered in the graveyard, talked, talked some more, and asked the deceased for forgiveness, explained to him why they hadn't come earlier—this was for monetary reasons—and then ended the session by firing a blank round into the air to pay tribute to him. Then they started looking for the grave again and, much to everyone's surprise, the contours of the grave were now clearly visible beneath the overgrown grass covering it. The deceased family member had accepted their repentance. When Kali Tchikati later found out that a high-ranking party member had participated in this ceremony, he flew into another fit of anger, convened a meeting of the party's Verification Committee and had the man in question duly expelled for fetishism and engaging in occult practices, and then later verbally lynched him on the radio. At that time, Kali really was out of control.

"I behaved in this way more out of obstinacy than because of some deeply held conviction," he added, interrupting as he did my train of thought, "and because I was afraid something was slipping away, that I was beginning to lose my hold over things. I became more and more dogmatic. This was the time when I organized that seminar that has since remained legendary for the harsh and merciless way in which I confronted you, and you know, I'd have had you expelled from the party had you been an actual member, a party that you'd shown no interest in joining under the pretext that it would have restricted your freedom. Following that seminar, titled 'Religious Beliefs and Animism: Impediments to Development and the Anti-Imperialist Struggle,' all the schools, all the hospitals and clinics of various religious denominations were nationalized as a way to demonstrate in a dramatic fashion the radicalization of our ideological struggle.

"And then my father died. And that's when the problems that would precipitate my downfall really began. Coincidence? Bewitchment? A curse? I'll tell you the whole story and you be the judge?"

He stopped talking so as to take a big mouthful of wine just like a swimmer inhales that last gulp of air before diving in. This time I was determined not to interrupt him so that he could make it all the way to the end of his journey in this strange story.

* * *

"And so, when my father died," he resumed, "I found myself once again face to face with my uncle. You know how it is with our covetous families that don't approve of the children inheriting all of their father's belongings, especially when the latter is wealthy. And when it comes to the wife, let's not go there, she's plain and simple dispossessed, and that's when she's not banned from the family home. And it's not that my father was rich, but he'd built a house and owned a car that, although old, was still running. And so when he died, my uncle asked that he be given the car so that he could use it as a taxi and help him feed his wife and children. Of course, I refused; the car was to remain the property of his widow and children. A family council meeting was held and did not end well. The family—and I'm talking now of the big African family—ended up splitting into two separate factions, one siding with me and the other with my uncle. In fact, the latter even left the village and settled elsewhere, adding a new branch to the family line in the process that will remain as unknown to us as some lost tribe in northern India. At the time, my uncle made all kinds of veiled threats, which I of course paid no attention to, as any good materialist and consequential rationalist would.

"Then, something unfathomable occurred two weeks after the family meeting. In fact, if this had happened to anyone else, I wouldn't have believed them. So there I was, running a few errands around town after picking up the car from the garage where I'd just taken it for a full service, oil change, and had all the fluids checked. The old thing had started right up and the engine purred like a brand-new one. Right when I decided to head home, cruising along at barely fifteen miles an hour in anticipation of a sharp bend, the steering wheel suddenly jammed. I pumped the brakes but they didn't respond and the car slowly crept forward. Slowly but surely, as if pulled by a magnet, the car collided with a palm tree. The whole front of the car was dented, the engine smashed up! And yet I'd barely felt the impact, not a single window had shattered and all the eggs in the basket in the truck were unharmed. You must admit that this made no sense! In order to make sure there would be no question as to the strangeness of what had just happened, I had a mechanic who, in the presence of a bailiff, and let me be perfectly clear, in the presence of a bailiff, inspected the brakes after the accident and not only found them to be in good condition but also working perfectly well! It was enough to drive you nuts! It made no sense and it wasn't normal. And let me tell you, that was just the start of things.

"Not long after that accident, I started getting terrible migraines; my eyes were constantly streaming, and then, no matter how you look at it, something even stranger happened, I could no longer read the letter 'R'! Breasts became beasts, terra was now tea, blurred pronounced blued, and of course there were a bunch of other words that no longer made any sense, such as Max, paxis, and so on. Now one can be color-blind and not be able to distinguish the differences between certain colors, one can even be blind and not see anything at all, but how on earth can one be blind or color-blind when it comes to one single letter! That made no sense. Of course I went to see a certified specialist, an ophthalmologist, and a neurologist as well. They couldn't find anything wrong with me. In fact, the answer to this, which I only figured out later, couldn't have been more straightforward: I'd been shot in the head by some sort of mystical, metaphysical weapon, one of those guns that only the witch doctors we have around here know how to make. And it was these invisible pellets that had struck my optic nerves and that were the source of my terrible discomfort.

"What really tested my patience though was the hunting accident I had. You know how much I've always loved to hunt. As a child I was always chasing after antelopes, hunting down buffalo, and even setting elephant traps with my father when we lived up in the Sangha rain forest region. Well, I still enjoyed it as much as ever. After my car accident and the onset of terrible migraines, I went back to my village to rest a little, you know, to recharge my batteries. One day, with a few buddies, we decided to go on a hunting expedition in the Mayombe Forest. Since I was such a good shot, they had me lead the way. Something suddenly moved up ahead in the branches of an okoumé tree. I aimed and waited. It turned out to be a large monkey, delicious game meat, swinging and cavorting in the trees. I loaded the gun and fired. As it hit the ground, the Cercopithecus let out a piercing scream, an eerie, almost humanlike cry. We searched for a few minutes in the thick undergrowth before coming upon a gruesome sight: the body of a sixty-year-old woman lying face down with a gunshot wound in the middle of her back. Ah, my dear Kuvezo, I was utterly dejected. Someone, and there could be no doubt about it, some witch doctor, was responsible for this woman's metamorphosis into an ape, in the way some men can transform themselves into leopards, to perturb me and see for yourself how they succeeded. I was now a murderer. Thanks to my connections and my place in the party hierarchy I avoided prison. The investigation report concluded it had been a hunting accident, and all I had to do was pay compensatory damages. After all these deals and ordeals and some considerable soul-searching, I had little choice but to conclude, in spite of my historical materialist and dialectic positions, that my uncle was the one behind all this.

"Besides, he never left me alone. Everywhere I looked he was there, haunting my dreams, interrupting my sleep. One night, when I was disturbed around four o'clock by the strange humanlike meowings of a big gray cat, I found him standing naked in the doorway when he was supposed to be a few hundred miles from the capital back in our village. It didn't take me long to figure out what was going on because of all the lessons from childhood, and even though I'd always been able to repress this, it now came rushing back: this was pure witchcraft. And this was exactly how they were able get around at night in their mysterious airplanes, able to cover such vast distances, crisscrossing the Atlantic between Africa and America in one night. I know, I know what must be going through your mind right now, my dear Kuvezo, that it wasn't that long ago I was busy persecuting people on a daily basis on the radio who believed such things, calling them backward, and that I'd had several party members expelled accusing them of engaging in occult practices, and so on and so forth. But the fact was that my uncle stood there right in front of me in his birthday suit, startled in the light like an animal caught in the beam of a hunter's torch! Ah! If only I'd been able to grab hold of him, I'd have wrung his neck on the spot, and that probably would have been the end of my worries. But out of panic, I shouted, started to scream, while my uncle made desperate attempts to escape the harsh light, changing into a dog, a cat, an owl, an old man . . . and when my wife and neighbors finally came to the rescue, woken by the ruckus, he'd vanished or rather found a way to make himself invisible in the way only witch doctors from around here know how to. My neighbors eventually managed to calm me down and my wife helped me back to bed after preparing a nice cup of soothing mansunsu tea.

"I burst into a fit of rage when I woke up the next morning and decided I was going to render harmless this threat to society. My credibility in the party could only increase if I arrested him, since people would see in my actions a sign of impartiality and commitment, an indication that I wasn't afraid to come down harshly even on my closest family members. And so, taking advantage of my position in the party, I had my uncle arrested for engaging in occult activities and witchcraft. However, I faced somewhat of a conundrum before the Revolutionary court. How could one begin to try someone for an offense that could not exist? As far as the party was concerned, witchcraft and other such mystical events did not exist. Besides, I had no strictly material evidence to support my claim against my uncle, except perhaps for the smashed-up car, which could hardly be considered proof of anything. I suffered the consequences of this, and I have to tell you that my standing among my comrades started to take a serious hit. A few even started, in private, to call me a fetishist, an animist, even! The height of irony! But that wasn't all, since I also had to be alert when it came to my uncle, who was furious I'd had him placed under arrest. I was truly stuck between the hammer and the anvil, the tree and the bark.

"Therefore, in line with my logical and consequential way of approaching situations, I had no other option but to preempt my uncle and catch him off guard before something serious happened. In other words, I had to fight him on equal terms.

"As it so happens, my dear Kuvezo, there was a precedent in our glorious party. After a student drowned in the waters of our great river, in a spot with a reputation for having the most fish, the local fishermen stopped going there because of a rumor that a mermaid lived there, one of those mystical creatures we know as Mami Wata, the mother of the waters, reputed for abducting swimmers, especially handsome young men, and bringing them into her underwater spirit world. To counter these fears that were responsible for the shortage of fish in the capital, we invited the head of state, president of our avant-garde Marxist-Leninist party, to follow in the footsteps of the great Mao, in other words to swim in these waters in front of the television cameras. Before the divers were sent in to mark off the exact area in which our president was to show off his prowess, and even though we didn't believe in such things, offerings of fresh eggs were nevertheless carefully laid out, without the people knowing, at the water's edge in the way that the fetishists had recommended. This was, as they explained, because the beautiful

Mami Wata liked eggs even more than she did handsome young men, and so that while our president would be swimming, she in turn would be sitting on a rock, her attention elsewhere, busy cracking open and feasting on the eggs. As I already mentioned, as consequential materialists, we didn't believe in such things, but we did it anyway because in Africa, my dear friend, you never really know . . .

"And so, I decided to fight my uncle on equal terms. The first step was to visit an old man whose reputation as nganda (the word fetishist did not fully describe the full extent of his know-how) was matched only by the campaign we had launched against him just over a year previously, right after that famous seminar I already alluded to. He'd been arrested, beaten, tortured (only as the result of a blunder, I should add) by overeager young militants. To make an example out of him, his home and fetishes had also been burned for good measure. I hesitated for a long time before I finally went to see him—and with great skill—dangling a carrot before him—I found a way to surreptitiously approach him to present my dilemma. Basically, I wanted him to neutralize my uncle.

"I was pleasantly surprised by the old man's readiness to help, given all the terrible things I'd subjected him to. After years of being in charge of men and women, there are no longer any secrets, and so I immediately understood the reasons for his good will. In his mind, he thought that the sanctions we'd imposed on him would be lifted if he helped out, and that perhaps even we would help him rebuild the home we'd burned down. That was fair enough. In any case, this was far from being a problem for us, since the party knew only too well how to destroy or rehabilitate someone just like that, in the blink of an eye, a quick dialectic sleight of hand.

"And so he suggested we meet around midnight, as one would expect when reckoning with the forces of darkness, somewhere on the outskirts of the city at a discreet location where no one was likely to bother us. I'd be lying if I didn't tell you I was a little scared; that's why I had a trusted family member, someone who wouldn't betray me, come along with me. So that was where we met up with the old guy, punctual in a way we're not accustomed to in Africa, leaning up against a clunky old car in which a young man sat behind the wheel. I felt somewhat betrayed because I'd made myself quite clear in asking that he come alone, but he quickly reassured me.

"'You have nothing to worry about—that's my son, he won't say a word. I brought him along because I don't know how to drive, and we need to travel quite far, because your uncle is so powerful that there's only one place where I'll be able to disentangle you from the net in which he's caught you, and that's on your father's grave.'

"I shuddered at the word 'grave,' because I didn't like the sound of this one little bit. But it was too late to turn back now. As the saying goes, if you spit into the wind, it only ends up back in your face. And I suppose it wasn't just any old grave, it was my own father's and he wouldn't wish me any harm. Knowing that gave me the courage I needed.

"The graveyard was about six miles out of town. We settled into the car, father and son riding up front, and my chaperone and I in the back, bouncing along uncomfortably on the sandy and potholed track, while the old bone shaker, seemingly devoid of any shock absorbers, rattled along somewhat disconcertingly. We eventually pulled over and his son stayed in the car to watch over it.

"The three of us lined up behind the nganda. If truth be told, this old fetishist was a good guy: full of concern, calling me 'chief,' guiding me competently in the dark, this darkness that belonged to him. My father's grave was quite far from the road, but we had no trouble finding it. All of a sudden I felt somewhat overwhelmed. At that precise moment I could no longer say for sure whether or not I believed in it all; my mind was too tired to make a decision either way, and so I just let myself be guided along. The nganda got out a torch and pointed it at the ground just to check there wasn't anything dangerous lying around—such as a snake, a scorpion, or red ants . . . —and then asked us to kneel down. He did the same, called out my father's name three times in the way one does on the phone, saying 'hello, hello, Father Kali,' and then launched into an incomprehensible speech, as if he'd all of a sudden been empowered with the gift of glossolalia. Finally, he repeated three times 'Yes, I understand,' turned toward us and said: 'Your father has confirmed that it's your uncle who's responsible . . . ' One last wave of materialism passed through me and I started to have a few doubts since I don't believe in life after death. I'd broken with what was one of the fundamental elements of African cosmogony, especially when it came to my own ethnic group, with that long line of descent, that long living chain that was the link between the founding ancestors and the elders, the elders and the children, that sacred chain that kept the dead among us the living, thereby freeing us from the metaphysical anxiety associated with death that those natives of Europe still have, that all-encompassing view of the universe that did not distinguish between the force that made the sap in a tree flow or man's penis rise up. For me, at least, all that was left of my father were carbon and nitrogen atoms, a few molecules of phosphoric acid. . . . I was fine with him confirming that my uncle had bewitched me thanks to his powers as nganda, but to claim that he'd actually spoken to my dead father, well, that was going too far, and I simply couldn't believe him. But I'd had no time to recover from the initial shock and I ignored the kernel of doubt I had about him as he proceeded: 'So as to undo your uncle's powers, you need to return to your original condition, that means you need to be naked.' We didn't think twice about taking off our clothes. He gathered them into a neat pile and placed them on top of my father's grave. The sky was starless and inky black.

"He shone his torch on a small pouch I hadn't noticed until then, revealing the contents: gunpowder that we called tiya tua Mputu, fire from Europe. He recited another litany and instructed us to close our eyes, which we did. We heard a match strike, and then total silence for a few seconds, the kind of silence you only hear in graveyards or that must have existed before the creation of the world, I mean before the Big Bang. And then suddenly a terrible explosion lit up the night sky and broke the secret and sacred silence in the graveyard. This startled us, we opened our eyes, and I swear on my father's grave, I've never been as scared as I was at that moment! The nganda was nowhere to be seen, and he'd taken all our clothes with him after igniting the gunpowder. We took to our heels, running naked all over the graveyard, stomping on the offerings, smashing crucifixes in our path, as all of my authentically African upbringing came rushing to the surface, everywhere I turned the spirits of the dead whose peaceful rest had been disturbed chased after me; I could feel their warm breath and shallow breathing down my neck. Fear-fear, panic fear. I was convinced my heart was going to jump out of my chest at any moment! And when, in the distance, I heard the car start, I understood that the fetishist and his son had abandoned us. As for my companion, I had no idea where his fear had taken him. I thought I'd gone crazy when I realized I was all alone in this big graveyard in the midst of darkness. I might very well have done . . . because I still couldn't tell you how a militia patrol, Revolutionary militants at that, found me the next morning wandering around the graveyard in nothing but my birthday suit, haggard and talking to myself, until I came to my senses at the sight of their weapons aimed at my naked self amid shouts of 'Your papers, comrade!'

"I'll spare you the details of what followed since you've probably heard all that there is to hear anyway given all the fuss the radio made of my expulsion from the party, a party I helped establish, and how in a quick dialectic sleight of hand they proved to our good people how I'd always been a reactionary even before the cradle. All that was left for me to do was to leave the capital, abandoning my wife and children, and go back to good old Pointe-Noire, my hometown. I started a small business to make ends meet, but it folded two months later. That came as no real surprise, given that my uncle is still after me and won't give up until I'm finally dead. So I'm just going round in circles. He wants to kill me, my uncle wants to kill me . . ."

Then he stopped talking and seemed relieved. I hadn't said a single word the whole time he spoke. Our glasses were now empty and all of a sudden I could feel a heavy silence. As a matter of fact it was getting late, and except for an old lonely drunk finishing off one more last glass of red wine, the bar had emptied out. It was as if we were actors on a strange stage enveloped by the night. The bartender had turned off the music as a hint it was time for us to be on our way.

"What do you make of all this, as a science professor?" He asked, breaking the silence.

"I really don't know," I answered.

"You don't believe me, do you?"

"The issue is not whether or not I believe you. . . . How shall I put it?"

"Everything in me refuses to believe all of this! Beginning with my Christian upbringing, then later my Marxist materialism. And yet . . ."

"And yet what?"

"And yet Africa is here before us, rising up, unexpectedly, almost inadvertently, at the very place we thought we'd laid it to rest. When it comes down to it, what is reality for any society? In the end, isn't it based on how it decides to react, to behave in accordance with its fundamental beliefs? Which comes down to saying that it doesn't really matter whether or not what it believes in happens to be true or false (if such terms still hold any kind of meaning), the essential thing being that this belief translates into some form of social, psychological, or cultural reality."

"Well that's quite different from what you used to say when you were the head of the party's ideological propaganda."

He brushed away my last comment, a little annoyed, as if I'd failed to understand what he was trying to convey. And then, talking to himself, he added, "My uncle wants to 'eat' me like the witch doctors do . . . You can or cannot believe it . . . but one thing is sure though, Africa has its mysteries . . ."

That's when he got up and left the bar, pulled away by the forces of the night. I wasn't sure why, but I suddenly felt all alone, and the anguish of the grave came over me. I quickly settled the tab and also threw myself into the night. The night was no longer welcoming as it had been earlier in the evening, but was now onerous, pulsating, a night reserved for cats that can see in the dark, for owls and birds of prey. I was scared and started running, my heart beating faster, in search of a taxi, eager to get back to the civilized safety and comfort of my hotel room. One thing was for sure, Africa had its mysteries . . .

A Day in the Life of Augustine Amaya

A violent gust of wind blew her wrapper against her thighs and almost knocked her over. She was forced to set her basket on the ground, rearrange her clothing and tighten her head tie, before grabbing it again and picking up the pace. It was threatening to rain, and at any moment the large drops that come with the end of the rainy season tropical storms would come crashing down. Even if she decided to run she wouldn't beat the rain; the Moungali roundabout near to which she lived was still a long way off! She loosened the knot she'd tied on the side of her wrapper and checked to see how much change she had left, a measly 75 CFA francs. She ran her fingers over the three metallic 25-franc coins, jingled them in her hand, hesitated for a moment, and what the heck, decided she would take the next foula-foula minibus that came along.

She'd had to walk over to the station because there weren't any bus stops at the customs office at the riverside port at Brazzaville's Beach. She tried to carry her basket on her head so as to free up her hands, but the wind was blowing too hard and so she had no choice but to carry it. She moved along as fast as she could, hoping to make it to the station before the storm started.

Would she have to come back again tomorrow all because of this wretched business of a lost identity card? She had no idea how this would all get resolved. She'd already made three trips to the police station, and three days in a row had to go home empty-handed. She'd gotten up at five o'clock that morning so as to be one of the first in line, hurried along as she always did and had made it there by a quarter after six. There were only two people waiting ahead of her. This was her lucky day, because the office chief showed up earlier than usual, right around ten o'clock. By the time he'd rustled through some paperwork, put away a few folders, and given out instructions to his subordinates, it was eleven; Amaya's turn came at eleven thirty. She secretly prayed that the chief was in a good mood.

"What do you want?" he asked, busy adjusting the medal attached to the lapel of his jacket bearing an effigy of the party's founder.

"I'm back again because of my identity card, which you've misplaced."

"I haven't misplaced anything," he thundered. "This is all because of your own negligence."

"But it was your office that made us hand over our cards and . . ."

"And what? It's your own stupid fault for obeying such absurd orders!"

"But . . ."

"But what?"

"Nothing, Comrade Chief sir."

"This whole identity card business is really starting to piss me off. I'm going to put an end to it once and for all."

He turned around to glance at the clock affixed to the wall. Her eyes followed the movement of his massive body, puffed out with authority. To the right of the clock hung the portrait of the immortal President, youthful and thick-lipped, dead-assassinated by she wasn't quite sure who, given all the contradictory versions she'd heard. The wall to the left was plastered with slogans that meant nothing to her for the simple reason that she couldn't read. The comrade chief turned back around, glanced at his wristwatch, as if he needed to confirm the time on the clock was accurate, and then mumbled through the mustache adorning his delicate mouth "that only ate meat," in the words of one of our most well-known musicians.

"Since it's already noon, why don't you come back around two o'clock."

"But sir . . ."

He slammed the counter window shut.

Amaya wasn't quite sure what to do next. She certainly didn't have enough time to go all the way back to Moungali, and in any case that would be a pointless waste of money; she really had no other option but to wait. She left the building and wandered along the jetty. Small vessels docked one after the other, unloading yelling, screaming women traders who argued with the customs officers. These men were the absolute masters of the place, grabbing hold of them, harassing them, barking orders, and lashing out with their batons when they didn't react quick enough; or they just confiscated their merchandise and only agreed to hand it back in exchange for some form of payment. The women were used to the beatings, to the slurs, insults, and outrages at the hands of these customs officers, since from as far back as they could remember, all forms of authority, whether colonial or postcolonial, reforming or redemptive, reactionary or revolutionary, or for that matter adherents of Bantu socialism or of scientific Marxist-Leninist socialism, had treated them with the same contempt. The very idea of a world in which all citizens, no matter whether they were men or women, would be treated with a little more dignity, compassion or understanding, was beyond their wildest imagination. And they were there each and every day under the scorching hot sun, pushed and shoved, having to be extra vigilant whenever a customs officer or other shady character came a little too close to their goods.

Amaya also made her living in the small-trade business. Taking advantage of the drop in the zaire on the black market, she would cross the river to Kinshasa and buy a range of products—butter, oil, soap, flour—to name just a few, and then sell them piecemeal that same evening once back in her neighborhood in Brazzaville, under the light of a candle made from a piece of cloth soaked in kerosene. During the daytime she would set up at the market next to the station where the best deals were to be had; but they'd recently been chased out of there, booted out by the soldiers, and then by the shovels and bulldozers, all because the market just happened to be on the President's new daily route. His security detail couldn't be bothered when it came to the livelihood of the little people. Her margins weren't great, but still enough to be able to feed the six kids she had left out of the eight her ex-husband had abandoned her with. One had died from malaria when he was only ten months old, and the other, a girl aged eleven, a Young Pioneer in the party's youth organization had been crushed by a tank during the annual parade celebrating the Revolution. After thirteen years of marriage, her husband had abandoned her for an improper wedding to a younger, more educated woman, one more worthy for a man newly appointed to a high-ranking political and trade union job after languishing for the past fifteen years in a dead-end office job. And so she'd had to fend for herself in a rental unit with six kids to take care of. Unable to read or write, but still with enough dignity not to turn to prostitution, which had become a common choice these days, she'd found the courage, and with the limited resources at her disposal, to try her luck in the retail trade. Her ex-husband, now a member of the avant-garde single party, was untouchable. Taking him to court in the hope of getting him to pay some kind of child support was out of the question, and in any case, given her level of education, she had no idea this was even an option. Hasn't phallocratic society always been this way? Men are free to seduce and abandon women. A husband could have several mistresses and no one would bat an eye, but if a woman so much as had an accidental lover she would be pilloried and driven out of the family home.

Another vessel pulled away from the landing, slicing the Congo River and leaving behind churning froth as it made its way over to Kinshasa, the yellow-and-green Zairian flag waving in the wind. Black-and-white feathered birds whose names she didn't know played in the water and the wind, following the boat, at times flying on ahead, and then back over the stern to dive for fish. She stared across the river into the distance at the capital of the former Belgian colony, proudly displaying its high-rises. Eventually she looked at the waters below her on which mats of white flowering water hyacinths drifted nonchalantly.

She asked someone for the time. "It's five after one, ma'am." She still had an hour to wait. She was hungry. She untied the knot in her wrapper, where she'd put 300 francs. She bought a small piece of cassava bread for 100 francs, roasted safous for 50, and ripe bananas for the same price. She went and sat under the Kapok tree adjacent to the customs hall and ate her lunch. Then she was thirsty, so she bought some heavily spiced Tangawisi for 25 francs and went to take up position in front of the comrade chief's counter. She was lucky to be the first in line. She started her wait.

At 2:45 p.m. the comrade chief arrived. Amaya secretly and quietly prayed that everything would work out this time; the alternative meant starvation for her large family. She hadn't been able to go over to Kinshasa for three days, and she'd exhausted her supplies; and it was almost the end of the month, which meant that the rent would soon be due. The landlords were an odd bunch. A civil servant could not pay rent for two months and they wouldn't say a word, they just blamed the state for only paying employees every two to three months. But when a poor woman trader was a few days late, they would threaten to evict her. Ah! Please God, make this identity card problem go away! What on earth were they thinking, changing the rules like this? In the past, we always held on to our cards for the return journey. Now we had to surrender it at the border custom's office. That's why, four days ago now, she'd left it at the office, as instructed, and then spent the day in Zaire before making her way back with her goods. When the time came to retrieve her card, it was nowhere to be found. They'd asked her to come back the next day, and then the day after that, and then the day after that one. They treated her as if she was responsible for its loss and this was preventing her from going about her daily business.

During the colonial era, it had been relatively straightforward going to Kinshasa, but today it was much more complicated and you needed all kinds of documents. Of course she understood the need for strict control over the crossings, because they'd explained on the radio how the Revolution was threatened by bourgeois bureaucrats (she still wasn't quite sure what that meant exactly), how it was under continuous attack just like Vietnam had been, and that it had to be defended. Perhaps misplacing the identity cards of poor traders was part of the plan to defend the Revolution. Who was she to disagree?

The service window opened. This startled her, rousing her from her thoughts. She approached the counter, hesitantly, doing her best to hold back the people in the line behind her that started to surge forward.

"So," the comrade in charge and party member growled once again. "What do you want?"

"I was here already this morning and you asked me to come back this afternoon; I'm here because of the identity card your services mis— . . . have not been able to find."

"Oh yeah, I remember. I just had a word about this with one of my deputies, and they're looking into it. Come back tomorrow morning. Next."

Amaya thought she was going to burst into tears, and she had to make a big effort not to. Another wasted day, another day of lost business! Will tomorrow be another day? Her legs felt unsteady as she left the building, and once she adjusted to the sounds and heat outside, she started walking slowly.

A gust of wind sent the leaves swirling in a kind of devil's dance. Amaya was suddenly reminded of her youngest child, a little girl who'd started a malaria fever the previous night. She'd given her a chloroquine tablet, but would that be enough to cure her? Worried, she hurried along, almost running, and arrived at the station out of breath.

All the foula-foula buses stopped there, blue monsters, large uncomfortable beetles that people stormed onto like when the doors opened to the movie theaters in Moungali. Two left, then a third one. She untied the knot in her wrapper and got out a 25-franc coin, then retied it; she made sure her wrapper was tightly secured around her waist and jumped into the fray. A hundred or so people were trying to board a bus that could hold only thirty. People were pushing and shoving, kicking and swearing at one another. She found a way to balance herself on the footboard, and as she tried to grab hold of the guard rail attached to the vehicle, the ticket controller shouted out "boré!," the code word signaling to the driver that he could leave. The tires screeched and the bus pulled away violently. Amaya was thrown backward, but her foot got caught between risers and she was dragged for almost thirty feet to the screams of horrified onlookers. She eventually managed to free her foot and landed on the hard asphalt while the bus continued on its journey, disappearing into the distance somewhere in the vicinity of the Monoprix store. She somehow managed to get up, picked up the pieces of her torn wrapper, dusted herself off, and wiped some of the blood from her scratches. A kind-hearted soul handed her her basket. She thanked her with serenity and gathered up the rest of her scattered belongings. The first drops of rain started to fall, followed shortly thereafter by a heavy tropical downpour.

Augustine Amaya secured her basket on her head and, with great dignity, her frail silhouette glistening in the rain, could be seen walking off into the distance in the direction of the Poto-Poto roundabout.

Will tomorrow be another day?

Old Likibi's Trial

1

Old Ikounga looked down at the poor dying animal. She was lying on her side, her tongue swollen and lacerated from licking away at the scorched earth in the dried-out valley in search of a drop of water. This was the worst drought he'd ever seen, and nowhere in the litany of folktales or in all the stories the ancestors and elders told was there any mention of such a severe drought ever hitting this country through which the equator passed. It hadn't rained in four months, and what made matters worse, the rainy season had arrived! And day after day, from six in the morning until six at night, a blazing hot sun! He poked at the goat with his foot, but she didn't respond. The bulging eyes were an awful sight, and the protruding bloody tongue was covered in a layer of sticky mucus that was beginning to attract flies. They were swarming, big, fat, bluish green, and hairy, and ran over her eyes, entered the nasal passages, and came back out her mouth. Old Ikounga looked down at the animal again—it was the last of his five goats—raised his straw hat, wiped his brow, and put the hat back on. He looked up. The beautiful alluvial plain through which the river once flowed had been reduced to cracked dusty soil. In the distance, as far as the eye could see, the savannah was dry, large areas of bare ground dotted with patches of grass. Each gust of wind kicked up so

31

much dust that you had to cover your face with a handkerchief. One small spark and all that would be left would be a handful of stunted shrubs. He had to hold back the tears. He trudged back up the hill that led to the village. There was so little moisture in the air that his skin felt as dry as an elephant's. By the time he reached his home, he was breathless. The whole village felt sluggish. Even the women who were usually capable of withstanding just about everything didn't have it in them to venture out into the fields. Like the men, they now lounged in the shade of the safou trees! In any case, nothing would grow. He slumped sadly into his deck chair. Why had this calamity struck Madzala, a nice little village with its houses made of mangrove wood and thatched with bamboo leaves, all carefully lined up along the main road?

The village chief had done everything in his power, put all his expertise to work, but to no avail. The government commissioner to whom the matter had been referred had even made a special visit to the village along with a team of international experts from the UN and FAO, but they weren't able to improve matters, and the white engineer in charge had left without finding a solution to the problem and therefore been unable to alleviate the villagers' suffering. Old Ikounga turned the problem over and over again in his mind. His entire groundnut crop was ruined, which meant a loss of over 20,000 CFA francs; and his little herd of goats had been decimated, as well. And of course he wasn't the only one facing such problems. The village chief, Old Mouko, had lost more than twice as much as Ikounga had. In fact, the whole village was ruined and there were warning signs of famine in the region. What was going to become of them? One person had argued that the best way to ward off such a curse was to sacrifice a human life, but this was unimaginable. In any case, the days were long gone when you could kill someone, just like that, without having a scientific justification. To sacrifice someone, you first had to be prove clearly, legally, and scientifically, that they were guilty. At least that was the rule since the last coup d'état that, after readjusting the revolutionary path, had imposed scientific socialism freely chosen by the people on all the villages. How then were we going to put an end to this calamity?

Old Ikounga couldn't stop going over and over all these problems in his mind. "Let's think about this a little more. This drought can't be natural because not even the white experts were able to find a solution. What's behind all this? . . . Now, let's see, the last time it rained was four months ago—what was going on on that day? Ah! That was the day Likibi's daughter got married . . . yeah, that girl he wouldn't agree to me marrying, or Old Mouko too, as a matter of fact. They'd danced the whole night away on the occasion. . . . But that doesn't seem right, though, because those were the days when it still rained every day, so they couldn't have danced away the whole night . . ."

He heard his neighbor shouting and swearing at a fly. Everyone around here was really on edge!

" . . . and yet, I clearly remember them dancing all night long, and that big storm that blew away Bakala's roof while he was in bed with his wife on the previous night. . . ." He racked his brains and then abruptly, in a sudden flash of inspiration, jumped up and slapped his forehead. "That's it, I remember now, they'd stopped the rain!"

He fell back into his seat after this sudden revelation; he replayed the whole scene over and over again in his mind. Even though he'd sworn not to join in any of the festivities or drink any of the wine served at Moukiétou's wedding, on account of the fact that Old Likibi had turned down his own offer of marriage, Old Ikounga hadn't been able to stop himself from wandering over there to see what was going on, to listen in, and take in every detail. Right when the dancing had started up, he'd spotted some ominous-looking clouds, and then there had been a few thunder claps and some rather spectacular flashes of lighting had streaked across the night sky. The evening was just getting underway, and it looked as if it was going to be ruined. What would they do with all these guests who had traveled from faraway villages? What would happen to all those demijohns of palm wine and pineapple, to all the chicken and lamb? The answer was not long in coming. Old Likibi was summoned. The latter was content, enjoying the company of his distinguished guests, savoring the pipe he kept for special occasions, having just completed his fatherly duties—right after the uncle, he'd blessed his daughter and his daughter's husband, poured libation and called on the ancestors to give the young bride boys, girls, and twins.

Thus solicited, Likibi rose, looked up at the sky, wet a finger, and held it up in the air to gauge the direction of the wind, and then pointed to the precise spot at which he was going to light a fire. A big wood fire was built, next to which he placed a bottle full of water, a mortar and pestle. He drove a broomstick made of palm leaf veins into the ground, pinned up a live toad (a big fan of rainwater) somewhere else. And then he uttered a few words only he understood, as women carrying twigs wandered back and forth, ululating, and chanting

O sky, stay as gloomy as you wish
But you, rain, stay up there . . .

Thirty minutes later, a light breeze could be felt, and the defeated clouds dispersed, carrying away the rain with them. Old Likibi went back to savoring his pipe among his guests. The dancing went on through the night, switching back and forth between drumming and traditional rhythms for the older folks and modern beats, reggae, pop, disco, and so on for the younger crowd thanks to a battery-powered turntable.

That was the last time rain had fallen on the village of Madzala.

Old Ikounga was still seated in his goatskin deck chair and sweating profusely. All he could think of were his dead animals, his lost groundnut crops, the parched land, Moukiétou's wedding, the unrelenting sun. That was it—Likibi shouldn't have stopped the rain on that day! He got up, a determined look on his face and with firm steps headed over to the chief's hangar. He walked in, wiping the sweat from his brow.

"Well, good morning, my dear Ikounga, have a seat," Chief Mouko said. "How hot it is," he added, as if by stating the obvious, his own wisdom might somehow seem all the more striking.

He was also wallowing in his own goatskinned deck chair, his sore eyes sweeping tirelessly over the scorched savannah. This drought had ruined him materially but also morally. Morally, because as spiritual leader of the community, he'd been incapable of solving this serious problem that now threatened their very survival. Wouldn't he be forced to step aside because of his failure to connect with the ancestors? Moreover, now that the job of village chief was a paid position, the state's designated appointee was the official interpreter in the villages of the single party's decisions, it was all the more crucial to hold on to it, a secure source of revenue and one that didn't depend on the vagaries of climate. He filled a glass with water from a small jar he guarded jealously close to him and handed it to Old Ikounga. He didn't think twice before accepting it, drank greedily, and thanked him.

"I can see something's bothering you," Chief Mouko continued, again making recourse to the obvious to emphasize his vast wisdom as spiritual leader.

Ikounga adopted a more serious attitude, as someone would who's spent quite a bit of time thinking about something, obviously weighing heavily what he was about to say.

"Chief Mouko, I've spent a lot of time thinking lately; this drought is not natural, there has to be something behind all of this."

"Well you're not telling me anything I don't already know Ikounga, I've been thinking this too. You know that my primary concern is for the well-being of the community; ever since this terrible situation fell on us, I can barely eat, and I can't stop thinking about all these people who've lost everything and about this famine that threatens us. I knew the day that white engineer left the village without finding a solution that this calamity was not natural, because the whites can't solve the problems our supernatural powers are responsible for. That means, as you put it, that there's something behind all of this. But help me understand you a little better: are you saying that there's something behind all of this, or someone?"

"Ah, Mouko, it's no coincidence that you're the chief! You understood immediately what I was getting at. Wouldn't you agree that . . . perhaps . . . what I mean is . . . that somebody could . . ."

"Ikounga," the chief interrupted him abruptly, suddenly remembering that he was also the party's representative in the village. As it so happens, they'd invited him to the capital when he was appointed—he was still filled with wonder at the experience—where, for a whole week, he'd been housed, dined, and driven around, given spending money, and all at the government's expense, undergoing what in official jargon is known as an "ideological bath." How, for example, thanks to the revolutionary ideology embodied by the party, one had to abandon superstition and retrograde traditions altogether, and forge ahead with modernity thanks to science . . .

"Ikounga," he had thus interrupted his interlocutor, "but surely you know we have to stop believing in evil spirits, in witch doctors, in the worship of ancestors because, as we were told back in the capital and hear all day long on the radio, science and scientific socialism teach us that there are no such things as evil, supernatural spirits?"

Old Ikounga didn't have to be reminded of this because Chief Mouko had, no sooner back from the capital, and following the instructions he'd been given, scheduled a meeting of the whole village to share with them the details of his trip. In fact, the meeting had been rather heated. He'd ordered the villagers to stop worshipping the ancestors, to destroy their fetishes because these were symbols of backwardness, to stop asking for dowries when their daughters got married and to refuse to pay them when someone asked for their hand in marriage and, for those who were believers, to stop praying: together, these explained why the country's economic liberation had stalled, why the crop yields had been so low, why the roads were in such poor shape, the prevalence of malaria and sickle cell disease, why so many women were sterile, and the list went on.

Likibi had been the first to jump in.

"Mouko, do you take us for fools? Have you forgotten you're speaking to grown-ups? They took you on a trip to the big city, you had a few nice meals, saw the city lights, you enjoyed the company of women, they gave you some money and a red medal, fattened you up like a big fat pig, and instead of leaving us the hell alone you had to come here and bother us with your bullshit stories. If the priests and all those whites who were here with all their mbouloumboulou colonial militias weren't able to get us to abandon the customs handed down by the founding fathers, well let me tell you that you and your little army of toy soldiers certainly aren't going to get us to."

Everyone had applauded. Mouko lost his temper.

"I represent the party and the government. I could have you arrested, I could have you put in jail, Likibi . . ."

"Come on now, quit the bullshit . . ."

"Do you know who you're talking to? The party . . ."

"Yeah, yeah. Your mama's party . . ."

A great hubbub ensued, and everyone was on Likibi's side, the village's true spiritual leader. Only Ikounga was on Mouko's side, but without being too visibly so.

"I'm telling you, no more fetishes, no more dowries . . ." shouted Mouko, and you could tell he was getting angry.

"Well I plan on marrying my daughter and collecting a dowry, and we'll see if anyone tries to stop me," Old Likibi yelled.

"And so," Chief Mouko continued, as if he'd not heard Likibi's defiant words, "if we want our arthritis pain to go away and to avoid accidents with the trucks that come to collect our crops, if we want the harvest to improve, our wives to remain faithful, well then the only thing that counts is scientific socialism. Henceforth, these are our new guides." He got out a photo of the President General, and then photos of two white bearded guys, so bearded in fact that you had to wonder how they were able to find their mouths when they ate, and then a photo of another white guy, bald this time, but with a mustache and small goatee, dressed to the nines in a three-piece suit.

"Have you lost it, Mouko? You expect us to replace our old white masters with new white ones? . . ."

"Hey, have you got a photo of General de Gaulle I could have?," one of the veterans, proudly wearing his World War II decorations, shouted out.

"And one of the Pope for me," called out some Christian guy holding up a cross.

Booed, exasperated, Chief Mouko had given up and had never actually had the courage to pin up these photos outside his home, as they'd asked him in the capital to do.

Yes, Ikounga remembered all of this only too well. He kept quiet a little longer and then, choosing his words carefully, reframed the dilemma confronting them.

"That's exactly what we've been taught. We need to eliminate, not hesitate to sacrifice in the name of progress and modernity anyone in the community who tries to impede our march toward . . . toward . . ." He couldn't remember the French word that described the thing, even though he'd heard it several times on the radio. "Toward . . . you know, that scientific thing that we all want, what's it called?"

"Socialism," Chief Mouko proudly responded, seizing another opportunity to shine, he who'd committed the word to memory.

"Yes, that's it. So, let me be clear, Chief, I don't care for witch doctors anymore than I do for fetishists, I'm all in favor of science. . . . For that reason, I can't help but think that if there were someone in the community refusing to abandon those backward practices that are preventing our soil from producing, the rain from falling and our country's march toward . . . toward . . . that thing."

"Socialism," repeated the chief.

Yes, that's it, if there were such a person in the community, we shouldn't think twice about eliminating them."

Chief Mouko scratched his bald pate fringed with white; his eyes wandered for a long time over the sun-scorched plain. In the distance, the wind and the dust were blowing. It would soon be time to put out all the little burning fires to avoid the risk of wildfire. He stood for a while in thought looking at the village and the hopeless crushed torpor and, scattered here and there, the livestock dying from dehydration and starvation. He remained quiet for quite some time, and then his eyes fell on Old Ikounga again. He seemed to have come up with a plan, although he felt a little uneasy with what he was about to say.

"To be honest, Old Ikounga, similar thoughts have crossed my mind. There has to be someone in this village engaging in fetishist practices, because this drought simply isn't natural. But I'm the chief, and I can't go saying anything—I have to be careful with what I say. That said, because you spoke of these things to me first and because you represent the party's rank and file, I can say publicly what I think. We certainly aren't the kind that vacillate when it comes to choosing between tradition and science. We're for progress and scientific socialism, as the new beloved chief of our single party of which I'm the appointed representative in this village has explained. If someone has to be sacrificed in order for it to rain, for the seeds and the plants to swell again thanks to the life waters, then this won't be because of archaic rituals but rather thanks to modern ways. Do you have anyone in mind?"

"Do you remember Moukiétou's wedding, Likibi's daughter?"

"Of course! She was the girl who turned you down."

"You too don't forget, and you're the chief!"

"Yeah well, that's not the point now is it. Yes, I remember that wedding. Now carry on."

"Do you remember why it didn't rain on that night?"

"Put it there," the chief exclaimed, slapping Ikounga's hand. "Enough said. We're on the same page. I can still see those big dark clouds filled with rain and promise like a pregnant woman's belly."

"Well, there you have it, it was Likibi who stopped the rain on that day."

"If it took me such a long time to denounce him, this was because, as the village chief, like I just mentioned, I couldn't very well be the first to point the finger at him. As chief, everyone is under my protection. But now that the initiative has come from the Party rank and file, my duty is to make Likibi's antiscientific practices known to all. There's no going back now."

2

According to the rumor mill, better known in these parts as bush radio, Old Likibi was going on trial! This said, many people weren't quite sure how to react to this news. After all, Old Likibi had been their spiritual protector for years, and not just in this village but for the whole region. He presided over all circumcision ceremonies, rites of passage, weddings, and all the ceremonies designed to reconnect with the ancestors. No one was old enough to have been there on the day he was born! But the rumor continued to spread. The latest was that Old Likibi had been arrested a week earlier and subjected to routine torture of the kind dished out in this country to all counterrevolutionary detainees. Some even said that he'd already been moved to the capital; according to others, because he was both a reactionary and pro-imperialist, this meant that he'd most likely transformed himself into a wind, one so strong that he'd blown away the prison gate and in the process managed to escape ... and so on. Old Likibi was going on trial, Old Likibi was going on trial!

The news eventually became official once the school teacher Konimboua Zacharie, himself a native of the village, was called on by the party's Central Committee, the right arm and precursor of the single Party, to preside over an exceptional tribunal. The thinking was that since Mr. Konimboua was a local, he wouldn't run into any difficulties enforcing the sentence imposed by the party's governing bodies. When it came down to it, he could hardly be accused of tribalism. They maintained that he was a certified teacher, but a few wicked tongues claimed he hadn't gone further than a basic preparatory certificate. No matter what was said, he clearly must have had some exceptional qualities, since how else could one explain his meteoric rise? Apparently, when he'd joined the party, he'd suddenly jumped from the rank of monitor to that of certified teacher. In any case, whether or not he was certified no longer really mattered, because when the Revolution was redirected after the latest military putsch, careerism and the cult of diplomas ended. So, as things stood, a garbage collector could become head of state from one day to the next, or a Private Commander in Chief overnight; what really counted was being red on the outside. And Konimboua Zacharie was red, all right!

And so one day he pulled up in Madzala in an official government Land Rover and, like any self-respecting progressive, was dressed soberly, without all the adornments typical of bourgeois bureaucrats, such as blazers, ties, cuff-link shirts, and likewise, paid no heed to all the clumsiness and hassle that characterized the reactionary and superstitious, such as those oversized African boubous that hampered your movements. Sober and revolutionary: a collarless khaki shirt progressives refer to as a Mao collar but that wicked tongues call toilet bowl, and pants made of the same material. He wore rubber sandals made from recycled tires, in the style of course of those Viet Cong from the days when they valiantly fought American imperialism. Spectacles, a briefcase overflowing with documents, and a portable, battery-operated transistor radio so that he would know immediately if fascist commandos, manipulated by imperialism, attempted to cross the river and overpower the Revolution that was in full swing, making advances day after day, each one more spectacular than the last.

Konimboua Zacharie was a relatively short man; he had several billhook scars on his face that reminded one more of the brutal tropical gulag side of the Revolution rather than its fraternal and generous side. He took deliberate steps, trying as best he could to convey an athletic appearance, but this really tested the buttons of his sober attire, which were already doing a heroic job of containing his bulging belly. Had it been anyone other than comrade Konimboua Zacharie standing there, one might easily have mistaken the roundness of his belly for the kind more typically associated with the reactionary portliness that betrays the lazy, bureaucratic, comprador bourgeoisie, rather than before a revolutionary stomach accustomed to the rigors and deprivations expected of scientific socialist praxis.

It was hot, really hot. The wind had started blowing again, and what could still be seen of the plain below was blurred by a veil of dust. Time was running out, and if it didn't rain soon, in addition to the risk of wildfires, there was a serious threat of epidemic disease because of the animal carcasses lying around, all the big, fat, bluish-green flies, and because of the wind that carried millions of airborne pathogens. Mr. Konimboua put on his polarized sunglasses before looking out onto the vast sun-drenched plateau. A well-nourished fly buzzed nonchalantly around his head, and as he tried to swipe it away he accidentally squashed it against his cheek, the look on his face expressing his revolutionary aversion toward this antisocialist insect playing provocateur. He got out his white handkerchief and wiped the spot where he'd crushed the fly. A group of rachitic children with bloated bellies that rivaled his own surrounded the vehicle.

"Where does the village chief live?," he asked with a revolutionary voice.

Impressed by the imposing figure, the children just pointed to the chief's hangar. He had deliberately not warned the villagers when he would arrive, so as to make sure they didn't organize a welcome reception that would have been tantamount to the crime of personality worship. He preferred to arrive incognito at the wheel of his vehicle like an authentic son of the people. He walked determinedly over to the chief's home. The chief had not been expecting him, and as he leapt out of his chair he saluted him and then offered him a seat on which he delicately rested his proletarian buttocks. He handed the important personality the whole carafe of water from which he drank delicately. He then made the following declaration:

"The party's Central Committee was persuaded by the arguments you presented them with concerning this affair. Concerted analysis of the situation facing our country shows that, if we're lagging, this is due to the mindset of our peasants who still prefer the hoe over the tractor, and cow dung to nitrogen-based fertilizer. We've made every effort to make them understand, through persuasion, slow and patient education, like moles tunneling, but still they refuse to adapt. And so now we've decided to make an example out of Old Likibi, to hold a trial that will be exemplary both procedurally and also in terms of the verdict itself. In this way the people will finally understand that we can use power as we see fit. As far as you're concerned, Chief Mouko, you've shown yourself worthy of the trust placed in you by the party and the government."

Chief Mouko was tickled to bits by the government envoy's compliments, and he wasn't really able to conceal his joy. He was then asked to bring together a group of his eight most trusted collaborators, which he did immediately. Mouko reiterated the facts once they were all gathered and the government envoy concluded in these terms:

"We have chosen the path of progress for this country, and for this Revolution to succeed, we must act mercilessly. We all know that Old Likibi is an important moral leader in this village and perhaps even in the whole region. But that's all the more reason why we must strike hard and at the very top so that the people understand that nothing can stop the Revolution. Go ahead and notify all the neighboring villages so that they can attend the public trial. The Revolution shall win! So, I look forward to seeing you all at seventeen hundred hours, socialist time!"

3

Dusk provided no relief whatsoever from the heat wave. Everyone was sweating profusely, doing as best they could to fan themselves, some with their hands, others using flyswatters or their hats. The eight judges, all men, took up position around the Presiding Justice. They were all clad in red robes he'd brought down with him from the capital. The room was packed and you could feel the excitement—folks were eager for a ritual foreign to any of their traditions to get underway. So as to emphasize the importance the government had placed in this trial, teams of workers had set up two power generators and affixed bright lights to the walls of the hangar where the trial was to take place. A crew from the radio station had turned up with all its equipment so they could broadcast the trial live all over the country. All of this activity was of course completely out of the ordinary for these simple villagers suddenly thrown into the national spotlight.

Master Konimboua, apparently certified, but who according to a few wicked tongues hadn't gone further than a basic preparatory certificate, now Presiding Justice of the Revolutionary court, struck the gavel on the desk to get the attention of the audience. The mood shifted to one of apprehension as instantaneous silence fell over the courtroom. Only the humming of the power generators, the faint squeaking of the recorders, and the occasional crackle of a microphone disturbed the silence. The villagers of Madzala really looked as if they were on another planet.

Presiding Justice: The court is in session. To the people present here today, let me be very clear. We are not gathered here to judge a man or an ethnic group or a region—what is on trial here today is the opposition to progress. The party leadership wants to demonstrate that natural causes alone cannot be blamed for our lagging development, but that in addition to the stranglehold of big business over our economy, it is the backward mindset of a number of peasants that is to be blamed. And when some of these backward folks will be publicly and mercilessly punished, others will get the message and throw themselves full throttle into modernity, under the stewardship of our avant-garde party. These are the reasons why we are gathered here today.

And then, with a look filled with that high degree of political consciousness and the fighting spirit the popular masses have always shown under the guidance of the single avant-gardist Marxist-Leninist party in power, he turned to the audience and shouted.

Presiding Justice: Will the defendant please rise. State your name for the court!

The wind had completely dropped and the humidity clung to everyone's skin. Likibi stood up in the accused dock where he'd been isolated far from everyone, and headed over to take the witness stand.

He clearly had no idea what was going on. He trundled along, chewing on a kola nut and came and took his place next to the Presiding Justice.

Presiding Justice: State your name.

Likibi (surprised by the question): What? You can't remember my name, Konimboua? Have you forgotten that I was the one who circumcised you?

Presiding Justice (doing his best to remain calm): Your name!

Likibi: Likibi.

Presiding Justice: Your first name.

Likibi: What's that?

Presiding Justice: Another name!

Likibi: Well, people sometimes call me Father Libiki, sometimes also Ta Ngudi because I am the father of twins. In fact you know them since you went to primary school together . . .

Presiding Justice: Let's stay focused, let's stay focused. Your profession?

Likibi: Oh, well, you know, when you've been around as long as I have, there isn't much you haven't tried your hand at. From palm wine grower to forest buffalo hunter. And I'm also a fetishist . . .

Presiding Justice: Fetishist! You said fetishist! Now listen to him! He's a fetishist! Don't you know that fetishists cease to exist when a country has chosen the path of progress? It's because of people like you, Likibi, that the country can't move forward. You're a reactionary, and you're going to pay dearly for that. Please note that, members of the tribunal. Fetishist, fetishist . . . Mr. Likibi, you stand accused of having taken part in acts of witchcraft, fetishism, and other reactionary activities during the month of January, practices that were all aimed at stopping the rain and with the intention of causing the country great harm and stalling in the process the country's march toward progress and scientific socialism, a prelude to communism and to the motto "To everybody everything according to his needs." Then, later, after your arrest and transfer to prison, you continued to engage in these practices by transforming yourself on different occasions into rotten papaya fruit crawling with maggots, into a snake, a gecko, and then finally into the wind itself, thereby eluding the vigilance of the guards. You were arrested only thanks to the dialectic reasoning of one guard, who, having spotted a rotten papaya fruit crawling with maggots, was brave enough to slam the door before running away. And still, thanks to the bravery of this same guard who, in spite of a nervous breakdown that lasted several days and during which time he had several nightmares in which he was being chased either by a boa constrictor or a dinosaur from prehistoric times, was eventually able to recount events to the party's authorities. These offences are punishable under articles 102, 103, and 165 of the Revolutionary Penal Code.

It was hot, really hot, the kind of heat you get during the rainy season except without the rain. The stench in the air from the animal corpses and the villagers themselves who were glued to this ritual foreign to any of their traditions, was as heavy as the atmosphere in the room. Presiding Justice Konimboua, known as Zacharie, removed his polarized sunglasses and continued.

Presiding Justice: Defendant Likibi, what do you have to say to these accusations?

The defendant continued to chew his kola nut.

Likibi: My son, I don't have anything to say, absolutely nothing!

The Presiding Justice gasped, glared at him, and his revolutionary mouth opened by itself. He was very upset!

Presiding Justice: I am not your son! Let me remind you that I am the Presiding Justice in this courtroom, and you will address me as Presiding Justice sir since you don't deserve to call me "comrade"!

Likibi: Oh my son, don't worry, I have no intention of calling you a "comrade"; I respect my age.

Presiding Justice: Mr. Likibi, in this context, "comrade" does not mean "comrade." This just goes to show the depths of your reactionary thinking. According to the revolutionary fraternity that unites us, us militants, comrade means comrade, in other words a comrade in arms and in the struggle, and you are certainly not my comrade, Mr. Likibi.

Likibi: Listen my son, I was there the day you were born and . . .

Presiding Justice: We are no longer living in the era of ancestor worship, Mr. Likibi; even if there was a time when I was your son, or at least a time when I allowed you to refer to me in that way, and even if I once called you father, I am no longer your son. I am now devoted body and soul to the socialist and scientific Revolution that will lead us toward horizons unimagined. So call me Presiding Justice sir, and if you don't, I won't think twice about holding you in contempt of court. Now answer my question: What do you know about these crimes?

Old Likibi had no idea what was going on. His hair suddenly looked much whiter and his face that much older. He glanced to his right and then to his left in search of some support from the crowd of villagers, more than half of whom he'd known since they were born.

Likibi: But I don't know anything about them, I don't even understand what you're saying.

Presiding Justice: People, I hope you are listening carefully: he claims he doesn't know anything. We are here to find out the truth, and we'll be here as long as it takes to get to the bottom of this. Likibi, do you acknowledge having fathered twelve children?

Likibi: Yes I do, and I'm very proud of it! And if the witch doctors had not eaten three of them, I'd have fifteen today.

Presiding Justice: Likibi?

Likibi: Yes.

Presiding Justice: Yes, Presiding Justice, sir!

Likibi: Yes, Presiding Justice sir.

Presiding Justice: Is one of your children called Moukiétou?

Likibi: Yes.

Presiding Justice: Yes or no, is she married?

Likibi: What, do you mean to say you didn't know she'd gotten married? We had a big party for her that went on all night.

Presiding Justice: Ah! You see, now things are getting interesting. Tell us what happened the night of this wedding.

Likibi: On the day of the wedding, as is the case with all weddings, there were lots of people around. I'm pretty sure the whole village was there, and some had even come from farther afield since as you must know and everyone else here today also does, the glory and exploits of Old Likibi extend way beyond the limits of this region. As a matter of fact, when the son of the secretary general of that association of yours . . .

Presiding Justice: I won't have you calling the party an association and especially in that condescending tone of yours as if it were some kind of band of outlaws! Watch your words!

Likibi: Yes, the son of the Secretary General of your party . . .

Presiding Justice: The party belongs to all of us!

Likibi: Ah? Me too?

Presiding Justice: Yes, even you, Likibi! Nothing comes above the party, and the party is always right even when it's wrong, because what may appear as an error today is in fact only the manifestation of one of the dialectical appearances of the phenomenon known as a contradiction. Our party isn't like those other parties in which everyone becomes a member at birth, but it's still the party for all citizens.

Likibi: That's right. So, when she got married, I was invited to come and bless the young couple, which goes to prove that . . .

Presiding Justice: Stop digressing. What happened on the day of the wedding?

Likibi: On the night of or the day of wedding?

Presiding Justice: They're one and the same! Do you think you're smarter and more educated than all these judges? Stop quibbling and tell us what happened on the night of the wedding.

Likibi: Ah, on the night of my daughter's wedding? I'm getting to that, I'm getting to that. So, as I was saying, the whole village was there, including folks who'd come from farther afield as I mentioned earlier, my son Presiding Justice sir. In fact, if you want proof of that, my uncle Moukalo was there, you know him, right? Everyone knows Moukalo is from the maternal branch of my family and that he's from the village of Mindzi, which is about 25 miles from here. He came with his three wives—of which one of them is from Komono, which as you know is 40 miles from here—his children, and the granddaughter of his first wife, because Moukalo, as you know, is in covenant with the Bakalas, who are another tribe and who live in the village of Dende over toward Mouyondzi. That's why the family fell out with him and why the tribe . . .

Presiding Justice: Will the defendant Likibi stop making a mockery of this court. That's twice now that you've used the word "tribe." I'm beginning to wonder whether you might be some kind of agent provocateur, one of those people who believe in a so-called African socialism when everyone knows that African socialism, in the same way that Bantu or Maghrebi socialism, is a sea snake just as fanciful as the Loch

Ness monster and that the only true socialism is the scientific kind discovered in the nineteenth century by Marx and Engels and later perfected by Lenin. Have you forgotten that the word "tribe" no longer exists since our Revolution was redirected, that it has been deleted, removed, crossed out, wiped away, erased, extirpated, and excluded from our vocabulary, and that since that salutary decision was made the results have been clear, and the country is doing much better because tribalism itself vanished along with the word. We are here searching for a solution to the main contradiction that exists in this country of ours and you, and all you can do is speak to us using a word that no longer even exists! Carry on like this and you'll see what happens.

Likibi: But you asked me to tell you what happened on the night of my daughter's wedding, and so how else can I do that without telling you about the family?

Presiding Justice: My comrades and I gathered here cannot see the point of all the twists and turns you're making, as if you were telling us the story of a Russian novel, needless to say a Russian novel written before the October Revolution; you know, one of those Tolstoy or Dostoyevsky bourgeois novels devoid of any proletarian lifeblood. The great Lenin himself didn't waste time reading Dostoyevsky's novels, and we're following his example. As immortal Mao—who will live on forever in our red hearts—showed us during his retreat from Yunnan, it is with the proletariat but also, and I insist on this point, it is also hand in hand with the peasants that we must create a national front that will encourage greater awareness among the masses exploited by neocolonialism, imperialism, and socialist-imperialism, while not forgetting social-democracy. Now these are the true problems, the true problems facing our country and Africa as a whole! For that which is well thought out can also be clearly outlined, as clearly as all these lightbulbs illuminating our night thanks to the generosity of the party. So don't go wasting our time with stories of the adventures and tribulations of your family. Do you think that our Revolution and our party are there to take care of such insignificant problems? So tell us about the night of the wedding. We couldn't care less about the cock-and-bull stories of your trib—... your family life.

Who was it that said Konimboua was not a certified teacher?

Old Likibi scratched his scalp studded with white hairs to try to get his strain of thought back. After the Presiding Justice's impressive outburst, he was now completely confused. He couldn't remember whether he was speaking about the uncle who'd married a woman from another tribe or the nephew who'd come to the wedding from the village of Makouba. Bewildered, he untied a piece of cloth he'd attached to his belt, took out a fresh kola nut and threw it in his mouth. It made quite a noise as he crunched into it and a spray of red saliva squirted out, and all the while he continued to massage his scalp. Presiding Justice Konimboua, known as Zacharie, jumped, furious, beside himself. Two buttons flew off and his belly was now hanging out over the waistband of his pants, which just made him even angrier.

Presiding Justice: Likibi, you're . . . Mr. Likibi, you're disrespecting the court, you're digging yourself a deeper hole, creating your own abyss in which you, the reactionary that you are, will end up being precipitated to the Apocalypse, toward the Armageddon of the final confrontation between you and us revolutionaries. Your neutron bombs and other scarecrows aren't going to frighten us. Stand up straight and take out whatever you have in your mouth, or you will be held in contempt pronto!

Dampness was now seeping through the revolutionary Presiding Justice's Marxist-Leninist Mao collar.

Likibi: I didn't know that chewing a kola nut would slow down the country's progress, my son.

Presiding Justice: I AM NOT YOUR SON! . . . I . . . I . . . Go ahead and swallow all the alkaloid and whatever other drugs are hidden in that nut, that's your problem, but I'm asking you to . . . to . . . Likibi, what happened on the night of your wedding?

Likibi: The night of my wedding?

Presiding Justice: NO! What has your wedding got to do with anything, a wedding that was probably celebrated according to obscurantist rites! I'm talking about the night of your daughter's wedding!

Old Likibi finished chewing the nut and swallowed the pieces he had left.

Likibi: Ah, you mean my daughter's wedding? I'm getting to it, I'm getting to it. Well, there were lots of people in attendance. I'm sorry you weren't able to come because you were also invited; but since you became important you've forgotten about the country, you've forgotten about the village. I slaughtered a sheep and three chickens and bought ten demijohns of palm wine with my own money. People were dancing and having a good time. And wouldn't you know it, the sky became overcast! This threatened to spoil the ceremony. So I grabbed my long pipe, the one handed down to me by my great-grandfather's father, and that I only smoke on special occasions and that I'll pass on to my eldest son. I smoked for quite some time. Meanwhile, Old Ikounga went to and fro with a big grin on his face; he was happy because he thought it was going to rain. He was very jealous of this ceremony because I'd turned down his request for my daughter's hand in marriage. He wasn't the only one, you know—I also turned down Mouko. How could I be expected to give my daughter away to old men like them, men old enough to have been her grandfather, even great-grandfather? Do they think that it's with their old worn-out blood that we'll achieve that scientific thingamajig you keep going on about? In fact, ever since Mouko came back with that medal your association gave him, he's been nothing but a pain in the ass.

Presiding Justice: Likibi, I'm warning you, watch what you say. You're saying disparaging things about two authentic revolutionary militants who've relinquished personal interests in order to devote themselves exclusively to the general interest. Let's get back to your sheep and chickens before I add a charge for slander to the already serious charges you're facing. What did you do after smoking your pipe, a despicable totem and fetish?

Likibi: That's when I made up my mind to stop the rain, my now Presiding Justice son. I sent the women off to fetch a mortar, a broom, green leaves, and so on. After the incantations, the women broke into dance, and the wind blew away the clouds off to the west. The moon reappeared and we went about dancing the night away. You really should've been there, my son Presiding Justice sir. That's all that happened. And then five days ago a group of young people came and took me away. They beat me and threw me in a prison cell and now you've come to the village and here you are saying all kinds of strange things that I can barely understand.

Presiding Justice: Is that all?

Likibi: That's all.

Presiding Justice: Defendant Likibi, I can't tell you how disappointed I am because you have told us nothing but lies! But the truth will shine through because our Revolution has nothing to hide and therefore has no reason to get itself entangled in a web of lies. Whether or not you're a tortoise with two shells, the spice of the Revolution will force you to reveal who you really are. This trial is being broadcast live, which means you can follow it whether you're in Washington, Moscow, Beijing, or in Bangladesh. We have nothing to hide. Now then, how many animals did you say you'd slaughtered?

Likibi: One sheep and three chickens.

Presiding Justice: People, you who are suffering so much because of the oil crisis and the inflation imported from capitalist industrialized societies, who are finding it so hard to make ends meet given the rise in prices in the supermarkets, you heard him, three sheep and one chicken.

Likibi: No, my son, now Presiding Justice, one sheep and three chickens.

Presiding Justice: Likibi, don't try and confuse us with your delaying tactics. Whether it's three sheep and one chicken or one sheep and three chickens, I'm a teacher, I know how to count, and no matter how you look at it we're talking about four animals. You don't need to have learned the theory of complex numbers or Boolean algebra to figure that out. Four animals for your daughter's wedding! Do you have any idea what that means? This means that you belong to the upper class, Mr. Likibi, to the class of those bourgeois bureaucrats who suck the blood of proletarians like us! Proletarians like us who bring home a modest civil servant's paycheck. But the Revolution is a class struggle and your kind will be annihilated. I'm going to let the other judges say a few words. My fellow Judges, I hope you will prove equal to your historic task. It is up to us to judge a representative of the property-owning and reactionary class that were once known as the Russian kulaks. In the name of the Revolution, don't think twice when it comes to de-kulaking just as one would de-rat. Now over to you. Judge Matanga.

Judge Matanga: Thank you, Comrade Presiding Justice. I would like to ask Defendant Likibi a question. Defendant, have you ever stopped the rain?

Likibi: You know very well Matanga that . . .

Judge Matanga: Just answer the question, yes or no. Have you ever stopped the rain?

Likibi: Just how old do you think I am? I was there when you were born, too. You know full well that I can stop the rain. My daughter's wedding wasn't the first time I stopped the rain, so why are you giving me such a hard time?

Judge Matanga was a little rattled and tried to regroup. The fact was, it was he, Matanga, now a Revolutionary judge, who'd been the one to go beg Likibi for his help on the day when his uncle's mourning was ending, a day on which it was threatening to rain and which would have ruined the ceremony. So he did his best to regroup as fast as he could.

Judge Matanga: Old Likibi . . . Defendant Likibi, don't get upset. Let's talk about something else, and please provide detailed responses. Is it true that you transformed yourself into a snake?

Likibi (laughing): No.

Judge Matanga: Why are you laughing? Didn't you transform yourself into something, not even a gecko?

Likibi: My goodness, the more educated you are, the dumber you become it would seem! Now that's enough. I can't tell whether you expect an answer from me or whether you're just trying to ridicule me Matanga. Everyone here today, even the children, know full well that Old Likibi cannot transform himself into a snake given that my tribe . . .

Presiding Justice (angry): Mr. Likibi, if anyone's backward among us, then it's surely you. Are you forgetting that Comrade Matanga is an eminent member of our party and that his presence here today has only enhanced the intellectual and ideological standards of this court. Take back immediately the word "dumber" you just pronounced.

Likibi: Konimboua, I was the one who raised you and now you're calling me backward! All the elders of the tribe here today and listening to us can be my witnesses.

Presiding Justice: Mr. Likibi, I've already warned you to refrain from using the word "tribe" because this word does not exist in our country. Instead, you can say "social group" or "linguistic-ethnic belonging," what do I know? In any case, you're lying to us, Mr. Likibi: the guard saw you transform into a snake. Using the dialectical and scientific theory of socialism, he can demonstrate by adding A to B that you transformed into a snake, then into wind, and finally into a rotten papaya fruit crawling with maggots. But let's be clear. Don't forget that this trial is a public trial and that as such you can have every expectation that you will receive a fair trial. I'm therefore asking you to be forthright. Likibi, do you admit freely and of your own volition, without any physical or mental coercion, that you stopped the rain four months ago during your daughter's wedding?

Likibi: Of course I do. Are you doubting my powers now?

Presiding Justice: Likibi, once again, you are not being tortured, you are free to answer as you see fit, do you agree that a severe drought like we have never seen has struck our country?

Likibi: That's for sure! In all my years I've never seen a drought like this one, and I wasn't born yesterday!

Presiding Justice: People, I don't see the point of continuing this cross-examination given that the defendant has admitted freely and of his own volition, without any physical or mental coercion, to the facts: 1) that he stopped the rain, and 2) that we have a severe drought like we have never seen before in this country. Now, you may well ask, what is the relationship between these two facts? Well (his tone became very serious) let us consider how dialectical reasoning could set about analyzing the problem. Let us begin by asking the following question: Why has there been no rain? Well, there has been no rain because it has not rained! Well, why has it not rained? Well, because someone stopped the rain. And who was it that stopped the rain? Well, Likibi, standing here right before you! So that was the first part of our dialectical reasoning process, thanks to which we were able establish a dialectical link between Mr. Likibi and the absence of rain.

Presiding Justice Konimboua took a moment to gauge, through his anti-imperialist and anti-obscurantist eyes that reflected the official party line, the impact of his argument on the illiterate peasants in the audience. Old Likibi, for one, did not seem convinced, but instead rather perplexed, like someone who was starting to have serious doubts concerning his interlocutor's mental well-being.

Presiding Justice: My question to you then is as follows: What is the consequence of there having been no rain?

On hearing this question, Old Likibi no longer had any doubt that Konimboua Zacharie had well and truly lost it. How else could you explain what this greenhorn down from the city thought he was going to teach an old hoary peasant who'd worked the land his entire life.

Presiding Justice: What is the consequence of there having been no rain? Consider these documents.

He opened his briefcase and pulled out several oversized manila envelopes, snapped it shut, and began exhibiting them one after the other to the audience.

Presiding Justice: What you have here are photos of the Sahel, well, look here at those scrawny animals, and over there at those carcasses, at that dried-out soil, all that sand. . . . Why do you think that is? Well, there is a scientific explanation for all this, and it has nothing whatsoever to do with ancestors or supernatural powers. People, so that we can all understand what we have here clearly, what do these ombrothermic diagrams tell us? Well, what we see is that the line for monthly precipitation is way under the one for temperature conditions, in other words, evaporation exceeds the pluviometric deficit. Well, people, this is what is known in vulgar language as a drought, a DROUGHT! And that's the problem in Madzala. The connection is perfectly clear. Why is there a drought? Because of the lack of rain. Why is there a lack of rain? Because someone stopped it. And who stopped it? Likibi. THEREFORE THERE IS A DROUGHT BECAUSE OF LIKIBI!

He concluded by thumping his gavel on the table. As if wowed by this reasoning, another button holding in the august personality's impressive belly popped off, which only further irritated him. He fell back into his seat.

Presiding Justice: Likibi, you may return to the bench, we will now proceed to questioning the witnesses; especially those who have observed you perform your fetishist, obscurantist, and antiscientific practices!

Old Likibi took out another kola nut from his waistband and started to chew it. He'd been at the stand for almost five hours, and his legs felt unsteady. He staggered back to the bench as quickly as he could, eager to rest. One after the other the witnesses took the stand. The court remained in session for a long time, as long as was necessary to extract any reaction from the people. Finally, they adjourned so that the judges could deliberate. It was getting more and more sultry, as it often does right before a storm. When they reconvened in the courtroom, the audience that had been prohibited from leaving were spread out willy-nilly on the ground. Some were fast asleep, snoring even. The sound of the gavel woke them all. Master Konimboua, known as Zacharie, Presiding Justice of the Revolutionary Court of Justice, had carefully rebuttoned his Mao-collared shirt, and read the verdict.

Presiding Justice: Whereas our country recognizes that people can stop the rain through fetishist, reactionary, antirevolutionary, and anti-Marxist practices,

Whereas it is also recognized in our People's Democratic Republic that people can transform themselves into monkeys, gorillas, snakes, the wind, rotten fruit, etc.,

Given the scarcity of rain, which no modern scientific or revolutionary means have been able to restore,

And given that this scarcity of rain has plunged the country in a deep economic recession,

The Revolutionary Court gathered here in Madzala on this third day of January finds the man by the name of Likibi guilty of stopping the rain throughout our territory with the goal of preventing the country from pursuing its revolutionary path that is being affirmed more and more, thereby making it harder for it to jump from victory to victory with each passing day.

The above-mentioned individual is also found guilty of transforming himself into a snake, the wind, a rotten fruit, and even perhaps into a chameleon openly and publicly, thereby violating the country's anti-fetishist laws.

The above-named Likibi having been found guilty to each of the charges, and in order to make it clear that the Revolution, wherever it is occurring, won't think twice to strike hard and at the very top, shall be executed at dawn.

And now, please rise and join me in singing the International.

N.B. According to the account of one villager from Madzala: When the trial ended, Old Likibi, a peasant from the village of Madzala, was moved, along with the power generators, the lightbulbs, the recorders, and the microphones, to the capital. He was never seen or head from again. After several newspaper articles criticizing him for having sold out to the forces of evil, calling him a fetishist, etc., the national radio announced on the morning of January 5 that he had been executed. But was he in fact shot, or rather tortured as a number of villagers be-lieve? Whichever it was, his body was never returned to his family.

On January 6, it still hadn't rained on the village of Madzala.

The Man

. . . *No,* this time he wouldn't get away! After a forty-eight-hour search to track him down, they had been able to retrace his steps, figure out his whereabouts, and locate the village in which he was hiding. And yet, there had been so many false leads! There had been reported sightings up and down the country as if he was somehow able to be in several places at once. Committed militants had apparently followed him deep into the inland region of the country yet weren't able to actually capture him; a special patrol had been parachuted into the swamps in the north and claimed to have seriously wounded him, all on the basis of a trail of blood that ended at the edge of a steep ravine; border guards swore they'd shot him in a pirogue that had regrettably tipped over and been swallowed up by the currents as he attempted to make his escape downriver. Unfortunately, further investigations were unable to substantiate any of these claims. The police beefed up security measures, a new branch of the police force was even established for this purpose, and the army was given carte blanche. Soldiers overran the capital's densely populated neighborhoods, burst into peoples' homes, stuck bayonets into mattresses stuffed with dried grass and cotton, slashed bags of fufu, hammered with rifle butts people who took too long to answer their queries, and didn't think twice about shooting anyone who dared to grumble at these home invasions. None of these drastic measures yielded the slightest clue, and there was widespread panic. Where on earth could he be hiding?

His exploit had been nearly impossible to pull off given that the nation's founding-father, the enlightened guide, savior, the great helmsman, president-for-life, commander in chief of the armed forces and beloved father of the people, lived in an immense palace that mere mortals were forbidden from approaching. And in any case, the 360-degree protection strategy designed by a highly qualified Israeli professor of polemology and counterterrorism was impregnable. Within fifteen hundred feet of the safety perimeter, soldiers had been positioned every ten yards or so and stood guard round the clock. These protective layers were repeated in concentric circles every few hundred feet from the palace walls. In addition to these security measures, a trench had been dug around the entire palace and filled with water, and was crawling with a population of African and Indian crocodiles, caimans imported from Central America that certainly did not live solely off alevins, especially during those times of repressive campaigns that regularly fell on the country after each genuine or simulated coup d'état. Then came the pit full of green and black mamba snakes, whose powerful venom killed its victims on the spot. The compound itself, a vast structure of brick and stone almost sixty feet tall was as imposing as the ruins of Great Zimbabwe, studded with watchtowers, searchlights, nails, barbed wire, and shards of broken glass. There were only two enormous gates that doubled as drawbridges and that had to be opened from the inside. And then there was the palace itself, the holy of holies, in which the dearly beloved father resided. No fewer than one hundred and fifty rooms in which a myriad of vast mirrors infinitely reflected everything and everyone, to such an extent that visitors couldn't help but feel uncomfortable or oppressed by this, only too aware that each and every gesture was carefully monitored. Every movement, as slight as it may have been, would, just like an echo, reverberate through each and every room until it finally reached the supreme mirror, the eye of the master himself watching over his universe. No one knew which precise room the founding president actually slept in, not even the expert hookers he called on often several nights in a row for his particularly elaborate pleasure sessions, and least of all the young sweet virgins he so enjoyed deflowering between promulgating decrees from his magical kingdom. However, if the beloved father-of-the-nation-supreme-and-elightened-guide-army-marshal-and-beneficent-genius-of-mankind was invisible in flesh and blood to the vast majority of his subjects, he was, for all intents and purposes, omnipresent: every household was mandated to hang his portrait in its entryway. Every radio news bulletin began and ended with one of his rousing messages. Televised news programs opened, featured, and concluded with his image, and the one and only local newspaper included at least four pages of letters from readers proclaiming their undying love in each and every issue published. Omnipresent but inaccessible. That was why his exploit had been all the more impossible.

And yet, he'd somehow succeeded in carrying it off: he'd managed to get into the palace, avoiding the crocodiles, the mambas, the Praetorian guard; he'd succeeded in thwarting the mirror trap and in executing the father-of-the-nation as one disposes of a common dissident or instigator of coups. And then he had simply followed his own footsteps back and left the way he'd entered, avoiding the watchtowers and the drawbridge, bypassing the green and black mambas, the crocodiles, and finally the Praetorian guard. And managed to get away! Forty-eight hours later he was still on the loose!

And then came the rumor, and no one really knew where it had started: they'd been able to retrace his steps, figure out his whereabouts, and locate the village in which he was hiding, and that he was now surrounded. No, this time he wouldn't get away!

Armored vehicles, jeeps, and trucks overflowing with soldiers had set out at three in the morning. The tanks didn't deviate from their course when they came to the houses in the villages they passed through, a straight line being the shortest distance between two points. Villages were set aflame in their path, crops destroyed, and the military vehicles left bodies in their tracks. They proceeded as conquerors vanquishing distant lands! They reached their destination in no time at all. The villagers were woken from their slumber with rifle butts. They ransacked their homes, emptied the granaries, looked in the trees, checked the crawl spaces. The man they were looking for was nowhere to be found. The officer in charge lost his temper, and the chinstrap on his helmet looked as if it was about slice his throat.

"I know he's hiding here somewhere, the one who dared murder our beloved founding president who will live forever in the pantheon to our immortal heroes. I know that this wretched rogue has a white beard and wears an eye patch. You have ten minutes to tell me where he's hiding, and if in ten minutes you haven't shown me to him I'll set fire to all your homes and torture and then execute one of you at random!"

The ten minutes elapsed amid a deep and anxious silence, much like those moments of silence that preceded the creation of the world. The officer in charge ordered that reprisals be launched. They brutally manhandled the villagers: some were strung up by their feet and whipped, soldiers rubbed red peppers over the open wounds of others and forced fresh dung down the throats of yet others. . . . None of the villagers came forward to denounce the man the soldiers had come for. So they set fire to all the houses and burned the harvest, fruits of a year's labor in a country where people barely had enough food to survive. And still no one came forward with the information they were after. This could be explained by the simple fact that they genuinely did not know the man who "carried out the coup."

The man had acted alone. He'd carefully prepared the attack over several months, reading, studying, planning; then he'd put on a false beard and covered his left eye with a black eye patch like the one pirates wear. He'd found a way to breach the impregnable palace and assassinate the great dictator. It had all been so simple that he'd sworn never to reveal his secret, even under torture. You never knew when it would again come in handy. He was nevertheless surprised to see the soldiers descend on his village. But had they really uncovered his identity, or were they just bluffing? From what he could tell, they had no idea who he really was since he was standing there right in front of them, surrounded by his fellow villagers, who for their part didn't have the faintest idea he was the man they were looking for. So there he was, upright, clean-shaven and with his own two eyes, waiting for events to unfold.

The officer in charge, a commandant, flew into a rage in the face of the villager's speechlessness.

"I'm going to say this one last time! If you don't tell me where this dickless one-eyed son-of-a-bitch who murdered our dearly beloved President for Life, founder of the party and leader of the nation is hiding, I'm going to grab and shoot one of you at random! You've got five minutes!"

He glanced feverishly at his quartz wristwatch and began the countdown. Two minutes. One minute. Thirty seconds.

"Mr. Commandant," implored the village chief, "we don't know this man and we can assure you he doesn't come from our village."

"Well, tough shit! I'm going to grab one of you at random and fire away. Maybe this will help you understand. Hey, you there, get over here!"

The commander picked him out of the crowd. He didn't seem surprised, almost as if he'd been expecting this all along. Deep down, he even hoped they would pick him, because he wasn't sure he'd be able to spend the rest of his days with someone else's death on his conscience. He was quite happy in fact, knowing that he would take his secret with him to the grave.

"You're going to be the innocent hostage we're going to sacrifice because of the stubborn nature of your village chief and fellow villagers. Tie him to a tree and shoot him!"

They kicked him, beat him with rifle butts, and slashed him with bayonets. He was dragged along the ground, then tied to a mango tree. His wife rushed up to him, only to be pulled away roughly. Four soldiers lined up and took aim.

"This is your last chance. Tell us where the assassin is hiding."

"I have no idea, Commandant!," pleaded the village chief.

"Fire!"

He briefly shuddered and then collapsed without so much as a sound. They would never find him now!

The smoke gradually dissipated. The village men remained in deep silence, shell-shocked, staring at the body slumped over the thick liana rope. The commandant, having followed through on his threat, stood before them, hesitating, not quite sure what he could threaten them with next. Rattled a little himself, he did his best to save face, at the very least to safeguard the honor of his military stripes.

"And so?," he eventually asked.

The villagers finally came back to their senses.

"And so what?," the village chief yelled back at him with contempt. "I've already told you we don't know the man you're looking for, you refused to believe us, and now you've gone and killed one of us. What else do you want me to say?"

The commander wasn't quite sure what to say. He swayed from side to side, uncertain, and finally barked an order at his battalion.

"Attention! Fall in! The search continues. That bastard might be hiding in the next village. Let's not waste any more time. Forward, march!"

Then turning to the villagers, he shouted, "We'll find that bastard, we'll ferret him out no matter where he's hiding, and then we'll rip off his nuts, his ears, tear off his nails, gouge out his eyes, and string him up naked in front of his wife, naked in front of his mother, naked in front of his children, and then we'll feed him to the dogs, you have my commander's word!"

The jeeps and the tanks started their engines and pulled away to look for "the man" someplace else.

They're still looking for him. They feel like they're close, that he's there, laying low someplace, but where might that be? The people's heart, crushed by the dictatorship, skips a beat faster each time someone mentions "the man." Even though the country is more heavily "patrolled" than ever before, even though the country is swarming with spies, informers, and hired killers, and even though he has appointed only men from his clan who are completely devoted to him to head every branch of the security apparatus, the new President, the second beloved father-of-the-nation entrusted with carrying out the sacred work of the founding father, doesn't dare go out. And even though, to ward off the threat, he proclaimed by decree that he was both unkillable and immortal, he still stays holed up in his palace, with its networks of labyrinths and mazes, mirrors and reflections, walled up since he will never know for sure when "the man" will suddenly appear and it will be his turn to be struck down, so that the freedom that has been stifled for so long can finally spring forth.

"The man," the hope of a nation and of a people who say NO, and who are watching . . .

The Ceremony

I'm a modest militant—I would even go so far as to say an exemplary citizen, publicly as well as privately, if that were not a contradiction of the quality I just mentioned a moment ago. The ceremony was scheduled to begin at nine o'clock sharp, but I was there right at seven thirty. If truth be told, it wouldn't have displeased me had the Secretary General of our one and only trade union noticed that I was the first to arrive, ready to lend a little hand here, to straighten the red flag's mast there, or even to dust off the portrait of our great immortal leader, ignominiously assassinated by the forces of evil—that is to say imperialism and its servants—or even just simply to brush off the red padded chair on which the President of our one Party's Central Committee, the President of the Republic, the Head of State, the President of the Council of Ministers, the Commander in Chief of the Armed Forces, the close companion and worthy successor to our founding guide, immortalized by his cowardly assassination, would later rest his revolutionary buttocks. No, it wouldn't have displeased me. But in the end, the only reason I was there early was because I was a sincere militant, fulfilling my obligations to the Party. Of course, I can tell you right now that I completely agree with the press release broadcast on the radio, which stated that the ceremony would be a political event. Ah! I haven't said anything yet about this historical occasion. Damn it, I'm never going to get my scientific thoughts straight as required by the dialectics of our revolution. Right, I'm getting to it.

In order to fight international imperialism and its servants, one must have an auto-managed and auto-centered development program (I learned these terms off by heart, because to join the Party you have to answer a bunch of questions of that nature to see whether you're a true communist and if you have carefully studied Marxist-Leninism). Now, to achieve this automobile development—sorry, auto-centered, we have to fight bourgeois democracy—sorry, bureaucratic (please forgive me, I learned so many things in so little time that it all gets a little mixed up in my head). In order to achieve this, one has to appoint competent and Red workers to run our factories. I myself, in all modesty, feel that I'm competent because for over ten years now I've been a guard at the factory, even if after all these years I still only earn fifteen thousand CFA francs a month. And for this ten-year period, there hasn't been a single infraction during either the day or at night. Of course, there were a few cases of embezzlement, and on one occasion the factory even had to close for a whole year because the former director, a member of the autocritic bourgeoisie—sorry, bureaucracy—had stolen two million three hundred thousand francs and seventy centimes that were earmarked for the purchase of spare parts and new machinery for the factory. He'd gone and built himself a villa by the sea. Our avant-garde Party, vigilant as it is, responded with a number of harsh sanctions: he's no longer a director here, but merely the director of some subbranch somewhere or other, even though, for humanitarian reasons, his villa was not repossessed (the poor guy has ten children, and he's the nephew of the Assistant Secretary General of our one and only trade union). My own honesty compels me to be straight with you and to let you know that, in a moment of counter-revolutionary weakness, I also embezzled funds that belonged to the national community, but I've now cleared my conscience and paid my debt toward society and the Party. In fact, after a one-year term in prison and after paying back in full what I owed for the three canned sardines, one of which was rotten, I'd "borrowed" one day when there was nothing left at home for the kids to eat, I was finally granted an amnesty the day our new President was sworn in, the man who restored democracy at the same time that he released some of the political prisoners arrested during the last attempted coup d'état, the one previous to the successful one that carried our leader into office. But I'm digressing. As I was saying, I'd been a guard for some ten years without there being any infractions at the factory. As far as I was concerned, that was proof enough of my competence. Redness was all that was missing.

When they first asked us to be Red, I wasn't quite sure whether they meant the color of our clothes or of our skin. Well, you know, I only got as far as the first year of elementary school, and I don't always grasp all the subtleties of political language. In spite of everything and through scientific reasoning, I managed to eliminate the color of the skin because, as I learned in the evening classes I attended to increase my chances of being appointed director, only the Indians, the Amerindians, not to be confused with the Indians from India, had red skin, and none of these creatures were to be found under our latitudes; it could therefore only be the color of our clothes. Besides, let me remind you that if these people are called Indians, it's because of Christopher Columbus's Eurocentrist ignorance, a man who headed west to discover the Indies as a way to increase the bureaucratic bourgeoisie's capitalistic and monopolizing profits, and had instead found America and its Indians. Whatever, it was the color of our clothes they were referring to, and in any case, it would have been racist to take into account an individual's skin color or tribal origin in determining whether or not they could join the Party.

I dressed up in red for an entire month. I went to work wearing a red shirt, red pants, a red scarf; only my shoes were brown and that's because I couldn't find a red pair. When the Secretary General of our one and only trade union, a member of the Party's Central Committee, visited the factory, I always made a point of blowing my nose with a scarlet red handkerchief so that he'd know that everything about me was red. In our country, the security services, that is to say our CIA or our KGB, often used women with somewhat questionable morality to extract information from people who were under surveillance. Well, every time I found out that one of them was spying for the State, I did all that I could to sleep with them, making sure that I always got undressed with the light on so that they could see that even my underwear was red! It wasn't because of debauchery or immorality that I cheated on my wife, but rather a sacrifice that I had to make to advance the revolutionary cause and its redness. On one occasion, after drinking a few glasses of red wine and exposing my eyes to cigarette smoke, my eyes became bloodshot. Everything about me was therefore red. I even had my bicycle repainted red.

To tell you the truth, I wasn't quite sure why they attached so much importance to the color red. I for one prefer the peaceful greenness of our forests, or even our turquoise blue skies that soothe the body and relieve the mind when it gets sultry outside just before a storm. Of course, I do like the bright red flamboyant plants when their flowers abruptly flower toward the end of the dry season, or rather at the beginning of the rainy season; but these flowers are beautiful because they break the dull blue-green monotony that characterizes the perennial leaves of the tropical forests, and also, because they only last a few fleeting moments. But let's leave the subjunctive out of this—sorry, I mean the subjective, and let's concentrate on the objective; it was worth liking the color red because if I was associated with this color, in addition to my competence, I would surely be appointed to the position of factory director, and, that would mean a salary increase from fifteen thousand to three hundred thousand francs a month! Ah! Let me tell you right away that the financial side didn't interest me at all, because I'm a modest, exemplary, and sincere militant.

For the month during which I was red, or at least thought I was red, I noticed how some people smirked when I passed them, how when they winked at me this was full of innuendoes, and then there were also the peculiar questions and riddles they asked, such as "What's got red eyes and rides a red bicycle?," almost as if they were mocking me. They were mocking me! My cheeks flushed deep red with anger when I finally realized that being red had nothing to do with the color of one's clothes, but that it was in the heart that one had to be red. And during all that time I was spending exorbitant and ridiculous sums of money, they hadn't said a thing! Of course, they were jealous of me; but, I told myself, I'll get them back the day when, having been recognized for my redness and competence, I'll be their boss.

So it was in the heart that one had to be red; I thought that was rather stupid, because everybody's heart and blood were red, even the invertebrate reactionaries—sorry, inveterate—that all the theocratic bourgeois are, no, auto-critical, no, bureaucratic (really, forgive me, I'm tired and I'm getting everything mixed up after a sleepless night). Well, after making inquiries and conducting extensive research, President Mao said that he who does not speak has no right to make inquiries—I understood that being red meant being a good militant, a good Marxist-Leninist communist. You see, I didn't want to let the job of director slip away over something so trivial. To go from fifteen thousand francs to three hundred grand a month, you didn't let that chance slip away: the good life, the women, the car I'd always dreamed of having, an Alfa Romeo or a convertible two-door Triumph, just like the one the Comrade Minister for Propaganda and Ideology drove. Of course, I hasten to add that, good militant that I am, honest, modest and exemplary, money and material possessions were not my main concern. I tell you this in all my simplistic militancy, and you can go and ask my fellow workers at the factory, I was a champion of faith, of the right path. You see, in these parts, there are these evil beings we call witch doctors. They move around at night through the medium of birds such as the owl or other birds of prey or in the form of strange animals like chameleons and tortoises and kill people by "eating" their souls. To protect ourselves from these evil spirits, we equip ourselves with powerful fetishes such as panthers' teeth, leopard claws. or various charms we get from Senegalese peddlers. We then say that we are shielded. I for one can assure you right now, that since some Party members were expelled for taking part in occult and fetishist practices, I no longer believe in fetishes and I'm against God because religion is the whiskey . . . the hemp . . . the onion . . . the tic-tac-toe . . . the pawn of the people. It wasn't easy for me to lose my faith in God because he'd helped me out a lot during some tough times, but in the end I had to choose and so I chose. And, to shield myself, I kept to the Party's symbols: I stapled a medallion with the effigy of our Party's founder on it to my red shirt. I glued the full-length color portrait of the current leader of our revolution onto the front mud flap of my red bicycle, and on the back one the coat of arms of our historic Party, which consisted of an intertwined hoe and machete garland with palm leaves, all against a yellow background. With that kind of protection, that kind of a talisman, I couldn't see how I could ever possibly be tempted by reactionary demons. My dedication was authentic, and I want you to believe me when I say that money and other material possessions were not my main concern.

And so I decided to study the teachings of Marxengels and apply for Party membership. Modesty aside, I must admit that I'm blessed with an intelligence that's a little above average, because even though I only got as far as elementary school, I still managed to master the Party's terminology in just one week. I listened carefully every day to what the journalists had to say on the radio and on the television, because in these parts, as the Comrade Minister for Information and Agitation had so aptly explained it, their duty was not to inform people about events and comment on them as they saw fit, but only to serve as propagandists for the correct line, that is to say as the Party's parrots. I learned everything by heart, including the slogans that plastered our walls, such as "To live is to produce" and "For the Revolution to survive, some ideas have to be censored." The most important thing really wasn't to understand what it all meant, but rather to be able to come out with one of those sayings at the right moment, either so that you would be noticed, or to silence an opponent, to be able to say for example, "Comrade, your attitude is that of a saboteur of the Revolution," and then sit back to watch him squirm as he pictured security agents already on his tail.

I also learned lots of new terms, and I can assure you, it wasn't always easy to understand what they meant. For example, it took me a while to know what a member of the bureaucratic bourgeoisie was. At first, I thought that it was a good thing to be, that you had to be one in order to live. Because on the radio they said that a bourgeois bureaucrat was an individual who drove around in luxury cars, who owned at least one nice villa, who had lots of money, etc., etc. What misled me was that when I looked around, I noticed that all our Ministers, our political tenors, the members of our glorious Party's Central Committee, had luxury air-conditioned cars, and their wives and children didn't have to bake under a scorching sun waiting for an unreliable bus to take them to the market or to school. They celebrated with champagne, they preferred imported beverages over local ones, and so on. And so I thought that all our revolutionary leaders were all members of the bureaucratic bourgeoisie, and of course I wanted to be a part of it too.

It was only later that someone explained to me that a bourgeois bureaucrat was a bad thing to be. Finally, thanks to my intelligence, which I told you about earlier, I was easily able to resolve this tricky problem. If you have two people in front of you and they both have luxury cars, a luxury villa, champagne dinners, etc., here's a foolproof way to tell them apart: the one who's a member of our single and historic avant-garde Party is a "high-ranking official" revolutionary and everything he owns, well those are just the basic material things he needs to be able to carry out his duties. And the one who isn't a Party member, well, he's a bourgeois bureaucrat, a comprador, an exploiter of the people, who has stolen all that he has from them.

From time to time, as I'm sure you've already noticed, all these phrases, all these slogans, all these terms learned at once created a kind of gridlock in my mind, but all in all, gridlock followed by a slight headache is better than missing out on a raise from fifteen thousand to three hundred thousand francs a month, isn't it?

But, big surprise, a new director was appointed, and it wasn't me! He wasn't even an insider! They really must think we're stupid, I'm telling you. After having drummed it into us for months on end that the new director would be chosen from among the company's workers, someone red and competent, they went and parachuted someone in on us they said was a proletarian because he was the son of a peasant and a Party member. Jeez, I'm also the son of a peasant! In Africa, we're all the sons or grandsons of peasants! Now, don't go thinking I'm just jealous because I didn't get the job, no, I'm honest, and after my initial disappointment, I looked at the situation and I saw that the Party was right and that the man was competent. Not only was he a guy the President knew very well, but they belonged to the same ethnic group. He could therefore only be competent. And so, to confirm my revolutionary sincerity and my lack of bitterness, I was there right at seven thirty to attend his induction ceremony, a ceremony that was scheduled to begin at nine o'clock.

I know that I've talked at length about myself, but I have yet to tell you anything about the ceremony itself. It was an historic occasion since, to inaugurate the new director's official appointment and to show how much importance the Revolution attached to the smooth running of our factories, the President of the Republic, President of the Party's Central Committee, President of the Council of Ministers, Commander in Chief of the Armed Forces, etc., was anxious to be there in person, before all the dynamic forces of the nation.

The professors were the first to get there. I don't know whether they're considered part of the commodore bourgeoisie, I mean comprador, but they were all there in their blue and wine-colored gowns. They looked like tunas in a shell. Professors are people I've always admired. I don't admire them quite so much these days, since they let themselves be publicly insulted by a student representative who, on the occasion of a somewhat ceremonial start to the new academic year, called them members of a class favorable to reactionary and bourgeois ideas and activities in his official speech. Not one of them had dared to respond. Our professors have become just like everyone else, officious, repeating the same slogans as us, the workers and peasants; they too just try to save their daily bread. Mind you, now that I'm about to become red, I'm not quite so hard on them, because I can see now how one has to start by rendering one's personality colorless, before one can successfully climb the arduous path to redness.

And so the crazy-gowned professors were standing there under the hot tropical sun. There were no chairs for them, only a few seats in the shade had been set aside for the important guests. The workers were next to arrive aboard buses that had been provided by the State, because they, they were the true dynamic forces of the nation, the proletarians who'd made the revolution, and I hasten to add immediately that I consider myself to be a worker. And then came the women and their revolutionary movement, the undertakers and their undertakers' revolutionary association . . . in short, all those who made up the dynamic forces of the nation.

Meanwhile, it was already ten fifteen. The ceremony was scheduled to begin at nine o'clock sharp, but you know, in Africa, time always runs fast; try as we might to hurry, time is always ahead of us. The workers, tired as they were, had scattered on the grass under the shade from the palm and Ravenala trees that adorned the place. The revolutionary undertakers had taken refuge in their black hearses. Everyone had more or less found a way to hide, at least for the time being, from the heat of the sun and to get off their weary legs . . . except for the professors, who, eager to maintain their status as the nation's dignified intellectuals and elite, remained standing under the scorching equatorial sun, sweat leeching from under the thick fabric of their medieval-looking academic regalia. As for me, well, I slipped into the shaded shelter reserved for the guests, pretending to pick up a chair here, a flag there, making myself in some way indispensable.

At ten forty five, the Comrade Secretary General of the trade union's car appeared, preceded by a two-man motorcycle escort. I can tell you in all honesty that I was the one who started the applause. The others, including the new director for whom this event had been organized, only started to clap long after me. Better still, taking advantage of my ten years of security work and knowing all the tricks of the trade, I got to the car before anyone else. I opened the door for him, he shook my hand before anyone else's, such that the photographer from our Party's revolutionary newspaper in which one only reads the truth, caught off guard, took several pictures, thinking that I must be an important personality.

I may have involuntarily held on to the Comrade Secretary General's hand a little longer than might have been appropriate, long enough for the photographer to get a good shot; but believe the word of a sincere, honest, and modest militant, I didn't do it for myself, but rather in the interest of the Revolution, so that people could clearly see that our Comrade Secretary General, though at the peak of the country's political apparatus, did not hesitate to mingle, converse, and live with the masses, even with the most humble little proletarian worker.

He went and sat in his place. Everything was in order, all that we were waiting for now was the leader of our Revolution.

Suddenly, we heard the sirens. The leader was coming. General commotion. People rushed, clapping, toward his motorcade. Dignified and competent militant that I am, I stayed where I was, because I'd succeeded in getting myself appointed in charge of the mike, that is to say I was the one who had to raise or lower it depending on the height of the speaker. At first they'd wanted to offer this task to one of the state security agents, that is to say to the secret service, but I managed to convince the supervisor of the ceremony at the factory that this job be given to an inside man, a model worker, a longtime employee, in keeping with the spirit of the occasion. I didn't have too much difficulty convincing him because he was a reasonable man, although in the end, since he was dithering, I had to slip him a thousand-franc note, not to grease his palm, but quite simply to thank him for having taken up his time. I've noticed how people, in our revolutionary country, I'm not quite sure why, always seemed that more diligent when you slipped them a little something. Are you wondering why the microphone was such an important responsibility? Well you see, when you're in charge of the microphone, you get to go up ahead of each speaker, you raise or lower the mike, and if need be you test it out. Imagine if this was for the President of the Republic himself: if you plan things right, you can get yourself in a picture with him. Do you have any idea how big that would be to be photographed with the Supreme Comrade! Find me a better way to get noticed! This is in no way opportunistic or an anarcho-profito-bureaucrato-situationist attitude. Put yourself in my shoes: I was competent, I was red, all that was left was for me to be noticed. And how? By militating, of course. Well, raising the mike for the President of the Republic was one way to militate!

Anyway, back to the sirens and the motorcade. And then there were the armed soldiers, in front, behind, on the sides. Oh, you know, everyone loves our President. As President Mao Zedong would say, he feels at one with his people, like a fisherman in the water, no, like a hook in a fish, no, like water in a fish, anyway, something like that. Armed soldiers? That was to stop the mercenaries who hide away across the river and in the forest, and who are recruited by the pluto-anarchic bourgeoisie, from coming with their remote control missiles and their neutron bombs, capitalist and anarchist devices, and attacking the leader of our Revolution. That was the only reason why he was accompanied everywhere he went by this cohort armed to the teeth. Of course, there were blunders! Like our buddy who, during a visit by one of our revolutionary leaders to the factory, got carried away with his enthusiasm and raised his arms a little too hastily to acclaim him. They'd thought he wanted to kill the leader and had opened fire. But one has to forgive our great historic army these blunders, because, you name me one country in the world where there weren't occasional police or military blunders?

The leader was coming, the leader came. Bravo. I was standing right next to the mike, as straight as a palm tree in the sun, chest thrown out, ready for the Revolution. The leader climbed out of his white, stretch Mercedes. Tall, dark and handsome, with a fine mustache, a soldierly appearance and impeccable poise, a man-of-the-people, a man-of-the-state, a man-of-the-Party, a man-of-the-masses, the incarnation of the Revolution, the President of the Party's Central Committee, President of the Republic, the President of the Council of Ministers and the Supreme Commander in Chief of the Armed Forces for life! The twentieth century could not not know this man! Our country may be a small country, but its leader was great! One cannot talk about France without mentioning Napoleon, about the Soviet Union without Lenin, China without Mao. Similarly, one will not be able to talk about Africa without mentioning our Supreme Guide, now standing there in flesh and blood right before my very eyes. And I recalled all those giant posters of our leader, his bust rising from a tide of hands reaching out toward him, his inspired look staring at a distant red star, guiding our people toward a glorious future . . . Ah! tears of emotion and revolutionary fervor ran down my cheeks! He took slow and calculated steps toward his seat before the ovations and hymns of praise, delicately positioned his Leninist buttocks in the padded red seat and crossed his legs. The ceremony could now begin. It was eleven thirty.

The Secretary General of our one and only trade union stepped forward; I rushed over to the mike and lowered it a notch, causing it to crackle when I flicked it to make sure that it worked, and stepped aside.

He started by saying that we had to fight against tribalism. That made me laugh, because the three of them, the Secretary General of the trade union, the new director and the President of the Republic all came from the same region. And to this day I'm still not convinced that I wouldn't be the director of this factory with three hundred grand in my wallet if I'd come from the same area as them. Oh, careful now, this isn't a criticism, it's perfectly natural that the country's leadership primarily consist of people who come from the same region and ethnic group as the President since, just like in a garden, some spots yield better vegetables and fruits than others. When a guy from my region was president, most political and administrative responsibilities were held by people from my ethnic group; now, it's the other way round. Nothing unusual about that.

In Africa you know, competence, like genius, always manages to suddenly flourish in the region or ethnic group of the person in power. I can think of a number of instances when exemplary revolutionaries had transformed themselves into inveterate reactionaries and vice versa a few hours after a coup d'état. But I'm digressing again, so let's get back to the ceremony. The Secretary General of our one and only trade union had already come to the end of his speech. He concluded by shouting at the top of his lungs.

"Long live the President of the Party's Central Committee, our President-for-Life until death!"

Of course, as eager as ever and taking advantage of the fact that my voice would carry as far as the mike, I enthusiastically bellowed out our Comrade Secretary's slogan.

"Until the death of our President, death to our President, death to our President . . ."

Then everyone took to chanting the same slogan, and with noticeable fervor over in the undertakers' corner.

"Death to the President, death to the President, death to the President . . ."

I noticed that the professors were not joining in, no doubt jealous that it was me, a simple worker with only an elementary education, that had started the chanting. In any case, they looked confused, as if they didn't know what was going on.

Anyway, these professors have always been against me. What proof do I have? Well, for a poetry competition that was held at the factory, we were asked to commemorate the pious memory of our late Founding President, and I wrote, in all modesty, the best poem of the whole bunch. Here are a few lines:

> O death Immortal
> fallen to the blows so mortal
> of the capitalist-imperialists

> Cell no. 5, in the red and
> revolutionary district
> will uphold for one hundred years
> the triennial plan
> toward auto-centered economic development . . .

Wow, check out the imagery, the allegories, the manner in which the word "Immortal," in its long strides, embraces and smothers the word "mortal" as if to repudiate it by dialectic association! Well, my dear professors on the jury didn't see any of this, and my poem was turned down. And so, the fact that they failed to appreciate my slogan today didn't come as a surprise to me. However, what I couldn't understand, was why the Comrade Secretary General of the trade union was darting these furious glances at me. All that I'd done was to take up his slogan. He grabbed the mike firmly from me, and shouted so loudly that for a moment I thought the loudspeakers were going to blow.

"President-for-Life, President-for-Life, for-Life . . ."

That's when I realized my mistake. I repeated after him immediately, with twice as much enthusiasm this time to make up for my slipup.

"President-for-Life, President-for-Eternity, our immortal President."

Finally, the Comrade Secretary moved out of the way, darting a strained smile at me. Phew, that was a close one. All this to say that all things considered, one should moderate one's enthusiasm.

The new director was the next up. He praised the Revolution and its leader. He urged the workers to do eight hours of work and not eight hours at work, because those who don't work have no right to a salary. Deep down I was thinking to myself, Yeah, buddy, I would have paid tribute to the Revolution just as well as you did if I'd been, like you, suddenly thrust into the position of director; anyway, keep talking my good fellow, we'll see what you have to say about us having to wait two to three months for our pay, does that mean that even those who have worked don't have a right to their salary? In any case, with three hundred grand a month without even counting the allowances, you probably won't even notice a few months without pay while us, with our fifteen thousand a month and our six kids! Of course, I hasten to add that I wasn't really thinking all this, I was just trying to imagine what a reactionary servile bastard, an unsound and animist imperialist might think of our comrade director's speech; because, as comrade Lenin said when he applied Marxengels' scientific discoveries, one has to fight erroneous ideas even before we are aware of them. That's why I think it is right to ban newspapers who don't think the way we want them to, and why I agree with the Party when its commission on censorship bans poets and writers from writing illegal verse or phrases. Finally, the Comrade Director General finished his speech by blurting out the usual slogans against imperialism, the acrobatic bourgeoisie and the general smoke screen that characterized the way State business was run.

Finally came the nail in the event, and to this day I continue to curse that nail!

The Revolution's guide, the man-of-the-people, the African Lenin, approached the rostrum, and I rushed over to raise the mike. I flicked it, the noise echoed through the speakers, everything was OK. I stepped aside to let him pass, slowly enough of course to make sure that I would appear in one or two photographs. Right when I was going to climb off the stage, at the precise moment I'd placed my right foot on the top step, the explosion occurred . . .

Even though I'd only had an elementary education, I do have some culture, and I can tell you that I can still see exactly what happened as if it was what film producers call "slow motion," which means—I have some basic knowledge of the language—flickback . . . backlift . . . backflash. When the explosion occurred, all the soldiers threw themselves to the ground, they lay down! The one time they weren't dealing with the poor terrorized civilians they descended on in groups of ten, armed to their teeth, ready to brutally search some poor defenseless guy's home before locking him up, they'd lost their usual arrogance.

It's not true what people say today about them "crawling forward in swarms." They were just petrified! As far as the professors were concerned, let's not even go there. I saw one of them, that chemistry professor who wears round glasses, has a beard and bushy hair, get all tangled up in his long gown. He fell over, tried to get up, fell over again, losing his mortar cap and his glasses. When he finally got up, he grabbed hold of his gown the way priests used to lift their cassocks in the days when they still wore them and started running as if the devil was on his heels. There was no doubt about it, he too was scared stiff! But what did I do?

Well you know, when I wanted to become red, I'd signed up for close combat and self-defense classes, because my dream, which I've unfortunately given up since, was to be one of the President of the Republic's bodyguards. Even if today I'm only a guard in a manure recycling factory, I've always aimed high throughout my short life. And so, when I heard the explosion and saw everyone take off, my heart skipped three beats. The revolutionary that I am, I forgot about my life, my wife and my six children, three of whom were just infants. The leader was there, all alone, a terror-stricken look in his eyes, torn between his dignity as the Commander in Chief and the Head of State, which told him to remain standing like Charles de Gaulle in front of Notre Dame Cathedral in Paris (I saw a film the other day at the French Cultural Center about the liberation of Paris because there were no revolutionary films about Lenin and the Russian revolution that week at the Soviet Cultural Center) and his desire to lie down and save his life. I'm telling you, I got a good look at his eyes, and believe me, he was in a blue funk. I hope that for that moment he experienced something of the anxiety felt at dawn by the poor innocent people whose execution he and his like order from their comfortable seats in their air-conditioned offices. It's true that might always makes right, and that all you need to be right is to have the guns on your side. But be careful now, don't go misinterpreting my words. If the Guide was afraid, it wasn't for himself, he was afraid for the Revolution, because, without him, who would lead our Revolution that was jumping from one victory to another? The leader was there, all alone. He wanted to shout out, "Help, guards!," but the guards were crawling forward in swarms under the stands or behind the seats. He ought to have shouted, "Help, my people!," and all the common people from the most remote working-class quarters would have climbed onto the platform to defend their leader as he stood alone in a panic. I was the only representative of the "people" left, and I did what my revolutionary conscience told me to do, I gave my body to the Revolution. I dived onto the leader and shielded him. Somewhat surprised, he tried to step backward and draw his gun because he always carried a weapon. As he moved, he got caught up in the wires leading to the mike, slipped and tried to hold onto the red cloth covering the platform. It ripped and he fell to the ground, landing on his presidential, revolutionary, and I suppose red buttocks. That's when the platform tipped, taking me with it, and I landed right on top of the leader. That's what saved me. Without the intimacy in which our two bodies were joined, me the guard at a manure factory and him the guardian of a revolution headed for glorious days and promising distant and happy tomorrows, the soldiers would not have hesitated to open fire. They didn't though, because they were afraid they might hit the President. In fact, firing was going on on all sides. As for me, they were pummeling me with their rifle butts, their boots, and who knows what else. With the arch of my eyebrows opened up and two broken ribs, I fainted and only came to in the investigating commission's torture chamber to the burning sensation of electric current running through my balls. Around three o'clock, they brought me a list with fifteen names on it and asked me to identify them as my accomplices. To be honest, I had no idea what plot they were talking about, but the pain had become unbearable. I therefore identified everyone on the list as my associates, and they were all immediately shot, after they had played a recording of their spontaneous confessions on the radio. Then, they hung me up by my feet, my head facing the ground, as a radio bawled out in the room.

Of course, forty-eight hours later, the investigation revealed that the explosion had been caused by a burst tire on a Renault 4 taxi and that the noise made by the puncture had caused the ensuing panic. But, as the government commissioner who presides over the Exceptional Revolutionary Court brilliantly demonstrated in a statement read over the radio that bawled out in the room in which I'd been tortured, there is no such thing as fate. Who asked this taxi to drive past at precisely the moment at which the President was climbing onto the platform? Why did the explosion only occur at precisely the moment at which the person in charge of the mike had made as if to step aside, if that hadn't been the signal they had agreed on? And even better, how did a nail, and an old rusty nail at that, an inanimate being, that is to say not endowed with autonomous will, come to position itself deliberately, pointing upwards, under the back left tire, that is to say the most heavily worn on the vehicle, without someone actually placing it there?

Was it not perfectly clear that the aim of the operation had been to profit from the ensuing panic caused by the deliberately provoked explosion and to kill the leader of the Revolution? And if there was no plot, why did one of the women traveling in the taxi claim to have nothing to hide when, after undressing her and systematically combing her body for the slightest piece of evidence, the security forces, living examples of revolutionary competence, discovered a large black beauty spot about a tenth of an inch in size on her right buttock? (I insist on the word right, he had exclaimed, because this just went to show to which side these people's political loyalties fell!)

To get back to the part played by the manure guard come sound technician, why did he when he showed up for the ceremony this morning—two hours ahead of time—on his repainted blue bike (Comrades, blue is the color of reaction, he had yelled, one talks of "blue blood" when one refers to Europe's degenerate nobility, exploiters of the feudal kind!), why then on that morning did he wave to one of the people he spontaneously identified during the interrogation as one of the accomplices who we immediately executed, someone he claims he has known for more than twenty years, if that was not an act of collusion? What was a copy of the French Constitution, a copy of the United States Constitution, and, listen carefully, a collection of articles on the despicable South African apartheid system doing among his books, if he didn't have some kind of secret and repressed desire to set up these regimes here . . . etc., etc.? Everything is jumbled in my head.

No longer knowing where I'm at, tired, famished, my body chapped after a night spent standing in a barrel full of salt lime water, I beg you, dear Comrade President of the Investigating Commission, tell me what I have to confess, what you would like to hear me say. Tell me who else I have to denounce as my accomplice. I'm ready to say anything you like, to sign any document. For pity's sake, even though I'm a revolutionary, a sincere, honest, and exemplary militant, there's only so much the body can withstand—I can't take any more!

Jazz and Palm Wine

The next day the spaceships landed. Art Blakey records
was what they were looking for . . .
LeRoi Jones (Imamu Baraka), Tales

1

They first appeared up in the sky as two luminous spheres spinning on their own axes like out of control night flies. After hovering for a while over a woman working in the field below they eventually landed very carefully close by. When she caught sight of the creatures that climbed out of the vessels, she took off in a panic, leaving behind all her belongings, including her donkey. The creatures, two of them to be precise, made their way over to the animal and with their hands covering their navels (a sign of respect where they were from), bowed their heads and then one of them pressed down the play button on the minicassette player he was holding. The phrase was spoken in Swahili.

"Would you be kind enough as to take us to your President?"

Now it was the donkey's turn to be terrified, and she wasted no time bolting in the direction of the village. The two creatures followed her, assuming she must have understood their request and was now leading them to the president of mankind. Meanwhile, the woman had already made it back to the village, out of breath, her shirt torn off, her face lacerated by the thorny branches in the bush she'd just ran through. She was screaming by the time she'd reached the village, calling for everyone's attention: "Hurry, hurry," she was shouting. "Flying saucers, strange beings! They look like humans but they're blue, steel-blue; their physical characteristics are similar to ours but they've got green hair! They have a jerky walk and they're really scary!"

The whole village was stirred to action. The children hid under their beds; the women were quick to hang up all kinds of charms and amulets and to seek refuge in their homes under their beds. As for the men, they grabbed their weapons, some their arrows or their bows, others their spears, while the veterans implemented the strategies they'd learned during World War II in the service of the motherland. They fetched their old rusty shotguns and took up positions around the village.

The donkey then arrived, braying. She stopped dead in her tracks, riddled with bullets and arrows. The two creatures also came to a stop and weren't given the chance to speak or to make the slightest gesture before they too were riddled with bullets, arrows, and spears, one of them falling flat on his face and the other flat on his back. Turquoise blue blood oozed from their wounds. Their dead bodies dried up almost instantly, turned to dust, and the blue dust quickly dissipated before the awestruck villagers. At the very same moment, as if the creatures that had remained on board had learned the fate of their comrades, the two spaceships lifted off and disappeared into the twilight.

2

Everywhere one looked, they were there, striping the sky, flashing their lights, dancing frenziedly, before landing on terra firma. There were literally dozens, hundreds, thousands of spaceships landing one after the other, the savannah of the Congolese Cuvette was blanketed in them, and they overflowed onto the riverbanks all the way over to neighboring Kinshasa. Those that fell into the river were submerged or engulfed by the waters, at first slowly, and then abruptly swallowed by the violent undercurrents that spat them back out onto the huge granite rocks jutting out of the water. Others exploded in a flash of light the second they made contact with the water, to the groans of the sluggish hippopotamuses and crocodiles, while the aquatic birds that had sought refuge on the large mats of drifting water hyacinths squawked from fear.

And they kept coming by the tens, hundreds, and thousands. The horizon as far as the eye could see was blacked out. They landed on Brazzaville, on Kinshasa. In Brazzaville, they crashed into buildings, broke apart, and went up in flames. Three fell on the presidential palace, went straight through the roof and crashed into the sleeping quarters before exploding. He ran for his life, grabbing his military uniform on the way out. They fell on the Soviet embassy and crashed into one of the city's main intersections. They fell on the National Radio compound, which was no longer able to broadcast because of interference from all the static buildup in the air . . .

Mayhem ensued.

3

The United States proposed what it called "saturation bombing," a system otherwise known as "carpet bombing," which had been tried and tested in Germany, most notably in Dresden, and later used in Vietnam. It wasn't by any means perfect, but too bad if a few natives died in the process. After all, not only had Earth kept rotating in spite of the massacre of ten of thousands of Indians, but America had even gone on to become the world's leading power. The Russians took the opposite view and favored a large-scale land invasion using tanks and armored vehicles, an old method they'd had some success with previously in Hungary, Czechoslovakia, and Afghanistan. Given the seriousness of the situation, China suggested it flood the Cuvette region with millions of men. Even if a few million lost their lives, there'd still be plenty left to stand up to the invaders who, when it came down to it, were little more than paper tigers. Cuba, with the support of Vietnam and North Korea, recommended guerilla tactics: if the invader moves forward, we move back, if he moves back, we move forward, that way we can gauge his strengths and his weaknesses. South Africa just came straight out and suggested putting up barbed-wire fencing, building a kind of apartheid line around the contaminated area and then defending it with soldiers of pure race. And, while they were at it, why not just go ahead and fill it with all the Blacks, all the Arabs, all the Chinese, and the Indians from America and Asia, all the Papuans, all the Malays, all the Eskimos . . . (his list was so long he had to stop for a moment and catch his breath). The delegate from Namibia pointed out that this corresponded to close to three-quarters of humanity, but the South African delegate responded that the gentleman from Namibia was using the term "humanity" rather loosely and that even if he were to accept the meaning the latter gave it, the sacrifice would be worth it if it meant saving the White race. The Afro-Asian delegates walked out of the negotiation room in protest . . .

They continued to arrive by the tens, hundreds, and thousands. The Congolese Cuvette was by now overwhelmed, as were Douala, Abidjan, Tenkodogo, Timbuktu. . . . They were now spread over the whole northern part of the continent and were also making inroads in the south and threatening the legendary mines between Katanga and Shaba.

It was still mayhem. The Soviet delegate accused the United States of having done nothing to prevent the invasion and even stated that he would not be the least bit surprised if he discovered that they were in fact behind all of this. The fact that the Soviet embassy in Dongola in southern Sudan had been hit ninety-nine times was only additional evidence to confirm his suspicions. The American delegate reacted by pointing out that their own embassy in Boko had also been hit. And in any case, it was a well-known fact that the Russians were hell-bent on sabotaging the work of the U.N. Security Council. And who knows, perhaps behind all of this was some big Soviet plot to Sovietize the world? May the Soviet delegate mark my words: "Better dead than red!" The delegate from Swaziland who was well-accustomed to the incessant quarrels in a harem, given that he had no less than four-teen wives and thirty-three children (including quintuplets), jumped in and interrupted the Russian and American delegates to remind them of the importance of this debate. In any case, it was pointless pontificating endlessly over the cause of this calamity because he'd al-ready consulted the spirit of the ancestors, who'd seen it all before, and from whom he'd obtained an answer. White racists had resorted to witchcraft as a way of wiping out persons of color, just like they'd done with the Yellow people in Song-My and My Lai, with the Blacks in Sharpeville and Soweto, and the Black Panthers in the United States. These words, transmitted live on United Nations Radio via the artificial Earth-orbiting satellite Terra 1, caused quite a stir in Harlem, where Black Power militants took to the streets brandishing portraits of Malcolm X, Lumumba, Nelson Mandela, and Paul Robeson. The French delegate, representative of the eternal champion of the Third World, of Africa for Africans and of Cartesian logic, warned the assembly against considering an exclusively U.S.-Soviet solution, which would be a greater potential threat to world peace than the one they were currently facing. With that as his starting point, he went about trying to convince folks of the good intentions behind their military interventions in Africa, but the boos from the Afro-Asian delegates eventually drowned him out.

And still, mayhem.

To the north, landings had been reported in Europe and America. In the Parisian suburb of Aulnay-sous-Bois, they'd fallen on Mr. and Mrs. Millet's small detached house. In Litchfield, a small town in Connecticut, they'd come down on Dr. Huvelle's home who, terrified, had rushed over to the house of his neighbor, an English architect, to seek refuge. They kept falling all over Africa: in the Central African Republic they coincided with the French intervention; on the island nation of Comoros during the assassination of the Head of State by a suicide commando that had sold out to imperialism. They were all over the Shana mines, and word had it they were beginning to drop in the Limpopo River . . .

The Belgian delegate insisted that an immediate decision be reached, or else NATO would act unilaterally. When the news came in that Johannesburg had been invaded, the South African delegate, who'd lost his previously blood-red complexion and was now white as a sheet, got up and declared that he was prepared to listen to any constructive proposal, even if it originated with a nonwhite. The delegate from Kenya rose and argued that, as dictated by African custom, the priority should be to identity the chief of the tribe of invaders. At that point, they should ask him to invite the elders among them to join him under the big tree in the village square, and that way chat over a few demijohns of palm wine. That would provide an opportunity to observe them closely.

The proposal was approved unanimously.

4

Absolutely! Jazz and palm wine. Palm wine made them very receptive (as corroborated by a recent study conducted in the Beaujolais Laboratories in France) and they sure loved to knock it back. As for John Coltrane's music, it initially threw them into a state of stupor that gradually eased toward a kind of nirvana (a Kathmandu Laboratory this time), which made them all the more receptive to the cosmic music and mesmerizing sound of Sun Ra (a collaboration between the Wernher-Braun Laboratory in the United States and the Gagarin Laboratory in Moscow). Nothing less would do! You could no longer harm them, pierce them, or burn them. . . . They cared neither for whiskey, nor water, nor women. Nothing! Only jazz and palm wine!

Millions of John Coltrane records were secretly stamped. Never had tropical agriculture or the palm wine industry known such a boon, and never before had soil specialists and agronomists been in such high demand. Everywhere he went, Sun Ra was treated like a king, and never had his Solar Orchestra been so busy.

5

The day of the party had arrived. To celebrate the tenth anniversary of the conquest of the Earth—the Great Conquest, as all the official records referred to it—all the presidents and heads of state on Earth gathered in the Congolese capital, point zero of colonization. The South African Head of State was given permission to attend the festivities so long as he promised he wouldn't attempt to shake hands with Sun Ra, a man everyone idolized at the time. In spite of his cries and tantrums, the organizers did not budge on that condition. Speech after speech exulted the courage, science, intelligence, wisdom, etc., of the conquerors come from Space without whom the Earth would never have been what it is today. The current head of the Organization for African Unity delivered the following great speech: "Us terrestrials, we are cultural hybrids on a cosmic scale, endeavoring to assimilate the best of two worlds. On the one side, the immense intellectual and scientific findings of our illustrious conquerors from the Universe upon which the suns of Vega and Sirius shine. On the other, we draw upon the terrestrial culture in which everything is based on the binary rhythm of the day and the night, a moonlight culture (devoted to love, sex, and other nonscientific activities) and a sunlight culture (reserved for solitude, alienation, and scientific activities)." And the speeches followed one after the other, given by captain-presidents, colonel-presidents, general-presidents, civilian-presidents, poet-presidents, and even poet-ministers. When the ceremony came to an end, it was time for libations. The leader of the conqueror's tribe reminded everyone jokingly that according to terrestrial legend there existed a god of wine named Bacchus. To show their respect for terrestrial traditions, they were going to honor this god by savoring the one really pleasant thing they'd discovered on Earth, namely palm wine. A terrestrial delegate jumped to his feet and said there was another no less important tradition on Earth that consisted in placing a nice wet kiss on the neck of one's host, which he promptly did. The leader of the invaders raised his glass and started to drink. Everyone then rushed the billions of gallons of palm wine freely distributed around the world. And they drank, and drank, and drank some more . . .

All of a sudden, from everywhere around, the houses, the inside of the Earth, from Space, the enchanting sounds of John Coltrane's saxophone reverberated. And the creatures started bobbing their heads, their eyes seemingly frozen. It wasn't long before hundreds of square miles of land were transformed into a mass of heaving bodies transfixed by a possession-trance dance rhythm. Even the President of the United States had to join in. He clapped his hands and pounded the ground beneath his feet with his cowboy boots, shouting out in his mother tongue "I've got rhythm, man! And soul!" As for the President of the Union of Soviet Socialist Republics, so as to not be left out, he took several grand Gregorian steps exclaiming "Tovaritch! Tovaritch!" That's when Sun Ra's rocket orchestra started playing. By the time he'd reached the speed of light, all that was not human had evaporated and vanished into Space.[1]

And then people began to dance with one another, to embrace and to sing to their newfound freedom. This is how Sun Ra became the first black man and jazz musician to become President of the United States. This is also why the best palm wine drinker of the year is appointed

Secretary General of the United Nations. And that's also how, when it came down to it, jazz conquered the world.

Epilogue: A year after this adventure, John Coltrane was canonized by the Pope as Saint-Trane. The first movement of his work *A Love Supreme* thus came to replace the Gloria in the Catholic Mass.

Note

1. Something happened right around this time and remains, to this day, unexplained: The South African delegate suddenly turned an immaculate white and the next moment evaporated. Several explanations have been put forward, but research on the matter has for the most part been organized around the following two questions: a) Was it the effect of the palm wine? Or b) Was he in fact a stranger in the terrestrial world? Until a plausible explanation is provided, a Verwoerd line (a kind of preventive sanitary cordon) has been traced around that country. This cordon is still there.

My Ghost Train

Ah, O Sun! I was dazzled by the sunlight as I came out of the laboratory. A beautiful summer's day in New York. Trees, green leaves, humidity, the smog sliding up the sides of the glistening skyscrapers and clouding the air under in the grayish sky. I feel the pressing urge to stroll all the way up to Central Park, but I'm short on time. The old daily grind, work, subway. . . . Junction. I can't cross because the light is green. Endless lines of cars slowly coursing through macadam arteries. The glimmering sun sends a blinding glare on the windshields. Ah, if only I had a pair of sunglasses like those movie stars wear. "OK, kids, hands up!" The cop, a big Irish fella busy chewing away at his gum, looks so funny stuck in the middle of all this trying to control the flow of traffic with his baton. The light turns red and I make my way across the street. Teller booth. There's already a pretty long line, as always during rush hour. The old lady ahead of me gets a few coins out her purse, a sad look on her face as she drops one and watches it disappear under all the bystanders. I smile at her. My turn. The guy behind the counter hands me ten cents change and two tokens without so much as a smile. I retaliate by not thanking him. I head for the stairwell and follow the arrow marked "Downtown." The farther down I go, the darker it gets, and I have to stop several times to let my eyes adjust to the light in the corridors. In the distance, the dull heavy sound of trains heading who knows where. I make it to the platform. Three benches up against the wall with two girls seated on one of them. Of course that's the one I decide to head for, and I sit down next to the prettiest of the two. She doesn't even notice me sitting there. I get up and move to another one and look back over at her with my best seductive smile. Nothing! Oh, and . . . In any case, I don't care much for blondes, I prefer brunettes. I give up. The station is filthy. Cigarette butts, old newspapers, beer cans and bottles. I look behind me at the sign on the wall: "No spitting." I feel like spitting on it. Farther down the platform there's a soda vending machine with a sign on it that reads "Be Sociable, Have a Pepsi." The station is getting crowded. An old lady pushes in front of me, she's got to be at least eighty, leaning on a cane, weak and weary. She smiles a ghastly toothless smile. I get up and offer my spot to the cute young blonde standing next to her. I love girls, especially blondes. At first she declines but then changes her mind. Oh women, never yes the first time around. La donna è mobile! My eyes wander freely over the walls. Ads and graffiti everywhere you look. I'm nearsighted and unable to read things that are too far away. I walk closer to check out one of the graffiti: "You're better off being a communist than getting married," ah, ah, ah, now that's a good one! I'm tired, I've had enough, I'm bored. I head back over to the bench I was sitting on. I slip on a piece of discarded gum that's now stuck to my shoe and damn near fall over. I scrape my shoe against the ground, but the gum won't come off. Disgusting. I reach the bench. The blonde girl I'd given up my spot to a while back sees me coming. I smile at her, she doesn't return my smile, she's already forgotten me. Ah! I hate girls, especially blondes. "Hey man, someone yells out, where's this train heading?" "To hell," I answer, kidding. He gets mad and starts cursing me. Asshole. Anyway, what do I care.

Now the station's completely packed. It's hot and clammy, like it gets in New York over the summer. I start walking again with both hands in my pockets. There's an empty can in my way and so I kick it. It rolls onto the tracks, making a terrible racket. Everyone looks my way. People are actually looking at me, paying attention. Finally, I exist! What a motley crew: some are wearing glasses, others not. I don't know any of them and I couldn't care less. Having said that, I'm generally quite fond of people, of liberty, democracy, socialism, justice, etc., etc. So, to be sociable, I head over to the vending machine. They're still watching me. I just love New Yorkers, they're great, I would die for them. I take a dime and slide it into the slot. Select my beverage. A paper cup drops down and starts filling with soda. Oh crap, the train's coming! I rush over to it, leaving my drink behind. The next sociable guy who comes along will get a free drink! Something for free in America! Life can sometimes be great for some folks! The doors open. The empty carriage inspires chaos. There's an incredible, ruthless surge forward, kicking, kneeing, and elbowing. God, I hate these New Yorkers! Constantly fighting for a place, for a place in life. The doors close. We're off. The train's sudden acceleration throws me back and a pile of other people fall onto me. Recovering my balance, I find myself face to face with the blonde girl from earlier. I frown and don't smile at her this time. Then I'm thrown up against her. I make the most of this opportunity and lean in, up against her and her firm young breasts. Another jolt throws me backward and when I bounce back there's someone between us. Ah, there's always someone or something between us and what we want most in life. C'est la vie, as the French say. One guy's poking me in the ribs, another's head bangs into mine. Now some big oaf of a man is crushing my foot under his shoe. I glare at him with all the anger I can muster. He mumbles some sort of half-hearted apology. The guy opposite me is trying to read the newspaper. A real acrobat! He's being pushed and shoved, people bump into him but still, undaunted, he continues reading his paper. An overweight lady over in the corner is snoring with her mouth open, sweat is poring off of her. I can't stand fat women, especially when they sleep in the subway with their mouths open. I'm also sweating now. The guy next to me stinks. The whole world stinks. I turn my nose and face the other way. Now I'm looking right at a guy who has a fairylike face. He has to be some kind of a clown. Or maybe just an actor, a comic actor. His brow is covered in sweat and it's running down his face, his mouth, smearing his makeup, mascara, lipstick, leaving green and white streaks. His face is now strangely multicolored. Where has his real face gone? I can see only his long eyelashes. His nostrils flare up as if he's short of air. Is he going to suffocate? He's looking at me. His mask scares me. A death mask. He's chasing after me. Please, mercy, I love life. I'm sweating more and more profusely. The tracks are squealing, the lights are flickering on and off. The Mask continues to stare at me as if he's going to grab hold of me, pull me into his nothingness. I try to close my eyes, no, please stop looking at me. The train is moving along again, I'm scared, I'm on the express train, a ghost train, a runaway train, a runaway train, going deeper and deeper in concentric circles, running, running, running . . .

A Love Supreme

IN MEMORIAM J.C. 1926–1967

> Jazz—Listen to it at your own risk.
>
> *Bob Kaufman*

1

When I ran into Splivie on that morning, his hair was disheveled and his eyes were bloodshot, his blank stare seemingly indifferent to everything and everyone around. He looked like he'd just rolled out of bed after a sleepless night and as if he hadn't bathed in a while. I knew that he'd been drinking again after quitting drugs—or since he'd regenerated himself, as he used to say playfully—but in any case, he was pretty cheerful after a drink, effusive. You could tell from his laugh whether he'd had a drink, a deep laugh that started with an alto-saxophone bass note, rose to a crescendo, slowly faded in a cascade of high notes and then died in a sharp snapping sound, would be a dead giveaway. But on this occasion, Splivie hadn't been drinking. He walked along with his head down, like an automaton, and seemed fragile, lost in this New York crowd in search of its daily bread. Had he started using again?

I overtook him, doing my best to blaze a trail through the crowd. I thought he'd recognized me when I finally got him to stop, and he did sort of gaze at me for a second, but then his eyes slipped away and wandered off into the surrounding void. I didn't give up, grabbed him by the shoulders, shook him, tried to make eye contact. But still, he didn't seem to recognize me and . . . he had tears in his eyes! Splivie was crying! Believe me when I say that there are few things sadder than watching a grown man cry, especially Splivie. I'd known him for years but never seen him in such a bad way. I'd been with him at those difficult times during the sixties when life in America had been hard to bear for people of our race. We were together on that summer's day when the Newark riots started and the police cornered us and opened fire on just about any black person who was moving and when, to avoid any unfortunate misunderstanding, we'd decided to lay down on the filthy burning hot tarmac, as still as possible, inhaling the cruel city's noxious fumes, listening to our hearts beating from fear while feeling our necks melting away under the scorching sun. We didn't dare bat an eyelid since the white cops with their conquistador jaws were looking for the smallest pretext to massacre someone. I was also there when Splivie came home to discover that his house had been completely ransacked and his little brother murdered, sprawled out on his living-room floor in a pool of blood. And on all those occasions, I'd never seen him cry or even really that sad. Only a look of indifference. It was as if the only emotion he was able to express was joy. Joy, happiness, and occasionally ecstasy when he listened to music. Indifference or joy, those were the two things Splivie's face was able to externalize. But never sadness. And as for crying . . .

I shook Splivie even more vigorously. He most likely was aware that something was going on, because his eyes flickered ever so slightly, and his lips, which I hadn't noticed until that point, were quivering. He tried his hardest to escape my stare, but I just shook him again, and finally he gave me a surprised look. He'd recognized me. He started sobbing and stammered a few words almost involuntarily.

"J.C. is dead."

I'm free-falling, sinking, diving, drowning, gasping for air, I'm suffocating, coming up for air, surfacing, I can feel hands holding me up, my heart thundering in my ears . . .

I finally managed to hold myself up without assistance; unfamiliar faces were looking at me curiously before continuing on their way, whereas Splivie, still with that blank stare, propped me up. What on earth was happening? What was I doing here? Suddenly it all came back to me. I listened to the violent and painful beat of my heart, and slouched over a little.

"That just can't be true, Splivie, please tell me it's not true."

"Yes, yes, J.C. is dead."

And he let go of me and walked away, his lips still quivering. Now it was my turn to feel completely disoriented. I had no idea where I was heading or where I'd come from, so I decided to head home. I was like a zombie, convinced I was about to choke in the clammy New York July weather. I was exhausted by the time I made it home, and the scene there wasn't a whole lot better. If truth be told, yesterday, Sunday, was my birthday, and I still hadn't had time to tidy up my apartment. Beer cans lay strewn about the place, tobacco and marijuana cigarette butts, half-eaten sandwiches, and already a few ants and flies had shown up—big fat ugly New York flies. I went straight to bed. Even Nancy hadn't had time to put away her things. Her bra and panties lay crumpled on the bed. On my reading table, next to the bed, stood the Agades cross I'd brought her back from Africa and her pillbox. I swept everything off the bed and hesitated for a moment as to what to do next. Finish off what was left of the bourbon and get drunk? I decided against that—waking up afterward is always so unpleasant, I'd be better off getting high on LSD, which I hated. I lay down on the bed.

2

The human spirit is such that, when confronted with overwhelming events, it will always find something it can hold on to. The problem was that the very thing I truly believed in had just vanished. Since I'd lost my faith in God, I'd pretty much dragged my spirit all over the place in search of the path that would lead me to knowledge, to some kind of greater meaning. That was how I'd discovered music. Well, actually, that's not completely accurate since where I come from, you're born with it. What I mean to say is that, thanks to J.C., music became something else, a means, a medium. It was more of a passion—it now had meaning.

When I first arrived in America from my native Africa, I had only a fragmentary knowledge of the classic music of Armstrong, Ellington, or even Bessie Smith, Scott Joplin, and a smattering of others. I liked it in fact and even had a couple of records. I found this music moving because it was nostalgic, and whenever I listened to these old tracks, invariably, images formed in my mind of large cotton plantations, steamboats at dawn making their way back up the Mississippi, and then all the cities, St. Louis, Kansas City, Chicago, and then finally Harlem and New York. When I felt down, I sought refuge in the haunting emotional power of Billie Holiday or Ma Rainey. And when the opposite was true, I skipped around to the more bravado and licentious rhythms of Fats Waller or Willie "the Lion" Smith. When it came down to it, this music was a kind of museum which I liked to delve into and discover the history of our people, but also an impasse. And what about Charlie Parker, I hear you ask? Well, quite simply, I hadn't heard of him. I would discover him only later, thanks to J.C., in fact. It was a shame, actually, since I became so accustomed to the new frontiers J.C. would transcend with each new recording that I never really got to fully appreciate just how revolutionary "Bird" had been.

This was also when I first met Splivie. When, where, and how isn't that important since the focus is on J.C. right now, and not on Splivie. Shortly thereafter I left New Jersey, where I'd been living, and moved to Manhattan, Greenwich Village to be exact. How time flies! It had already been five years since, one evening, with nothing better to do, we'd decided to go over to the Village Gate to listen to and check out this "New Thing" that people were starting to talk about . . .

I was starting to feel a little drowsy in spite of the stifling heat when I heard the front door open. It must have been Nancy coming home. I heard her rummaging about in the fridge, grabbing a Coke bottle, uncapping it. She'd made herself comfortable and was wearing only her underwear when she came into the bedroom . . . Nancy was so beautiful! I won't say anymore so as to avoid repeating all those age-old clichés that are used to describe pretty women. But there really was something about her all the other pretty women in the world didn't have, and her name was for me inextricably linked to J.C.'s. Our fingers brushed against one another for the first time listening to him play tenor saxophone on "In a Sentimental Mood" with Duke on the piano. By the end of the track we were kissing. From that moment on we'd been inseparable and spent every cent we had looking for rare copies of the records by the man who had brought us together.

"Nancy!"

She stopped, surprised to find me there lying on the bed.

"What are you doing here at this time of day? Are you sick?"

"No. . . . Yes, it's made me sick."

"What's made you sick?"

"Nancy, J.C. is dead."

In slow motion, she sank to the carpet and passed out. I leapt out of bed in a panic, but she regained consciousness fairly quickly and was immediately angry with me.

"J.C.'s dead and all you can do is lie there doing nothing! Lie there like some good-for-nothing!"

She hurled her glass of Coca-Cola against the wall and continued to yell at me, screaming. I couldn't really see what I'd done wrong. She was shouting, throwing everything she could get her hands on, and then started chain-smoking without paying any attention to me. She eventually settled, sat down and started crying.

I called Michael Fiator in Washington, a buddy of mine from Dahomey, but his wife answered and told me he was out. I tried to reach Archie Shepp in France but was informed he was at a festival in Châteauvallon. As a last resort I called the poet Imamu Baraka, but he'd left Newark the previous evening to give a series of lectures in California. It was also too early to get in touch with the people I knew in New York, since they were most likely still at work. And so here I was alone with Nancy—we were all alone. I got out all the booze we had left and started playing our J.C. records. We sat there listening. Listening? No, we were the music and that music was J.C. We finished all the bourbon that was left, and then I started on the gin. I was a little fuddled but still lucid. I was drinking in the music while Nancy, her head resting against my thighs, had drifted off. J.C.!

3

Ah! J.C.! I was with Splivie when I heard him perform for the first time at the Village Gate. I can't quite remember what he played, but it had been a long, very long piece, such that by the time he'd gotten to the end of it, the room had almost emptied out. The few spectators that had stayed on clapped weakly, and even then! Someone in the audience shouted out, "That'll teach you, maybe next time you'll play something shorter!" J.C. was devastated. He put his saxophone away and was getting ready to leave. He looked so sad, so alone! We decided to go over and show our support and I'm not quite sure how this happened, but the three of us ended up back at my place. I lived just around the corner, right on Bleecker Street, almost across the street from the Village Gate. We sat down, and I gave them each a beer, which was all I had to offer them.

"I really liked what you played," I said, "and you should not let what happened tonight discourage you."

"Oh," he laughed. If I got discouraged that easily, I would have gone back to Miles a long time ago. But how do you get this across to people? All that is alive must evolve, for God's sake! People need to understand that I'm constantly changing, looking for something different from what I was playing six months ago, three months ago."

"You were great in Miles's quintet," said Splivie.

This seemed to annoy J.C.

"You need to stop fixing me. I'm an artist, a creator. I have to keep pushing myself further. I need to evolve, live, do you understand? If I created my own band, that was because what I was doing before wasn't enough for me anymore."

Splivie tried his best to make up for what he'd said.

"As it turns out, the public only really wants to hear things that are familiar, or at the very least doesn't care for things it doesn't understand."

"To hell with the public," I interjected. "Just play what satisfies you."

"Well, you see, my problem is that I haven't reached the point where I'm satisfied with what I'm playing, and that means the public is even less satisfied than I am. Do I even know in which direction I should be going? So they aren't entirely to blame. Some of the blame is also my own."

He kept quiet for a bit, and then, thinking out loud, continued.

"I'm nothing without the public because my music is for the people. I'm willing to take into consideration their tastes so long as they're prepared to give me the space to explore what satisfies me . . . Ah, all this is very complicated indeed."

"Maybe the easiest thing would be to just give them what they like, and then play what makes you happy in private. After a session, for example."

"No, no!," he reacted passionately. "That would be completely hypocritical. A musician, a creator must only share what he feels inside, authentically." His voice had become heated, passionate. "There are already too many fakes in this world, too many frauds. Relations between people are so false, money spoils everything, and sincerity is discouraged if your goal is to be rich and powerful. And so what is left for us, what is left for me, anyway, what I have left, is my art, my music. Let's at least fight for it to remain pure."

His voice vibrated with emotion, and he was starting to scare me a little because I thought he was maybe possessed. Ah! J.C.! Only later was I fully able to understand just how challenging it was for a musician to express in words what he was feeling. We sat back and drank in silence.

And then, to my despair, Splivie blurted out, "Perhaps the public would appreciate you more if your solos were a tad shorter."

Contrary to what I expected would be J.C.'s reaction, he didn't seem overly bothered and responded calmly.

"I've thought about this, but you see, I just can't. I takes me at least fifteen minutes just to get going, to feel prepared for what I really want to express, and then I need another quarter of an hour to wind down. That's why I just don't get it when they say that my solos are too long. It would be just like telling me that the saxophone is a string instrument—it just makes no sense."

"Well, it certainly takes a lot of courage to go back day after day to the same place and perform in front of a hostile or at the very least indifferent audience, like the one you played to tonight."

It took him a while before he responded, then a fleeting smile appeared on his face. He emptied his can of beer.

"You found them hostile tonight? Well you haven't seen anything then. I'll never forget a particular jam session at the Birdland. I really felt 'on' that night. I was really 'into it,' blowing, blowing, almost as if I could see the notes coming out of my saxophone, I was pulsating along with them!" He was now standing and acting out the scene. "And when I finally reached the end of my solo, I gave the chorus a signal: nothing, not a sound! The whole crew had walked off the stage, disgusted, so it seemed. There I was, by myself, completely alone, and all of a sudden I felt naked, vulnerable, ridiculed standing there in front of everyone. The final blow came when one of the other musicians, the one I really looked up to, shouted out in front of everyone, 'Well, if that was jazz that guy was playing, then I wonder what the hell I've been playing all along!' That damn near killed me. I didn't step back on a stage for a whole year."

No one said a word. We just sipped away at our drinks in complete silence. Then J.C. started up again, speaking to himself.

"But I won't give up! I need to find a way to give to my listeners, to make them hear, see all those marvelous things a musician like myself feels in the universe. I need to make them feel the love of the world, a love supreme!"

His voice was vibrating again, his eyes sparkling. I couldn't help but think he must be possessed. He turned toward me, impassioned.

"You understand me, right? You know what I'm after . . . Drugs kill you, alcohol debases the mind. Women? Forget about them. So what's left? Music. You understand me, right? Only music can save me and maybe even help me to save others. My goal in meditating through music is to open myself up to God, which means to everything—to the love of the world, to that of mankind, to open myself to the sun, to vibrations, to cosmic energy. This will make it possible for me to elevate others, to inspire them so that they can attain their full potential to live meaningful lives. Surely you agree that there is meaning to life!"

He threw out that last sentence like a dare. Perhaps even to the universe. And that's where good old J.C. left us. Without saying good-bye, he slammed the door behind him as he walked out.

He didn't do another concert, nor did we catch sight of him for six months. It was during that time that I met Nancy and we began our wild hunt for his records. In reality, he was far better known than he'd led us to believe: he'd cut a record with Ellington, not to mention his recordings with Miles and a long list of other great classical musicians, such as Johnny Hodges, Thelonius Monk, and so on. But for him, those didn't count—they were in the past. He felt very strongly that music, like any living art, has a duty to constantly go beyond what was already there, to surpass itself. A deep connection existed between music and the rest of the universe, the kind of relationship one finds between energy and matter in Einsteinian physics. And so he always endeavored to forge ahead, leaving in his wake all those musicians who lacked faith, and even further back all those audiences stuck in their ways and content with their empty clichés . . .

4

And then, all of a sudden, J.C. returned! Believe me, as long as I'm on this earth, I'll never forget that moment. We learned on the radio, by pure coincidence, that he was scheduled to perform that evening. Nancy called Splivie to see whether he'd heard. He hadn't. I called my friend in Washington to ask him to jump on the next flight, but once again his wife, Joan, answered and informed me that he was away, on a business trip to Ethiopia. And so we reserved four tickets, for Nancy, Splivie, Muriel, and myself. Muriel was really beautiful, the epitome of the so-called black beauty. In fact, I'd nicknamed her Angelica—little angel—based on a number by that name she was really fond of in a rendering by J.C and with Duke on the piano. As it turns out, I'd always been in love with her. With her long Afro hairdo and glasses, she looked every bit like Angela Davis during the '60s. I was never really able to sit down and talk with her and certainly not to woo her. And to think that I was the one who introduced her to Splivie!

Our table was close to the podium for the musicians, and we were enjoying our drinks—you had to order drinks in the club—waiting for them to arrive. It wasn't long before they appeared. We applauded raucously and J.C. looked our way. I wasn't sure at first whether he recognized us, but I had the feeling his face was saying "patience, my friends, get ready for what you're about to hear!" Normally, the jazz clubs we went to in those days in America were noisy places. People shouted, banged their feet, clapped their hands, chatted away, drank, and smoked along with the music and the musicians. Which is pretty much as things were that evening when they started playing, in spite of all the emotion we felt at seeing J.C. again. Gradually, slowly at first, then rising, surging, erupting, and eventually submerging everything around like a torrent, J.C.'s saxophone emerged from the chorus. I swear, the whole room suddenly went quiet and there was absolute silence. The barman stopped in his tracks with a customer's order in his hand. Another listener stood still, his hand clasping the handle to the bathroom door. Everything stopped, actions caught in time, sentences interrupted and a concentrated and tense silence. J.C. was standing there in the middle of the quartet like a possessed high priest. Sounds, phrases, harmonies, passions, exclamations flew out of his saxophone, as inexhaustible as ferocious waves pounding against the rocks. The notes chased one another, caught up, blended, ran on ahead, such that one had the impression of listening to clusters of sounds sliding against each other, elementary particles escaping from an inner core in fusion! Harmonic components repeated incessantly over and over again almost simultaneously and with different intonations, almost as if he was playing two, three saxophones on parallel octaves at the same time! The fervor grew, grew, and became so intense, so captivating that the movements of the fingers became indistinguishable given the speed at which they were moving up and down on the scales of the instrument, faster it seemed than the speed of light. In this fervor, the man and the music became one in a vortex of sound at its purest: a nebula that explodes in the universe, outside of the realm of time and the clocks of mankind, in a universe in which all things become passionate and burning, where everything has become essence, where a star expires in a titanic explosion filling the galaxy with a thousand bright lights, a thousand little suns. We no longer existed. We too were transported on this journey along with the Master, the witch doctor: a great pagan feast, a Dionysian feast, hell and damnation, sulfur and salt, love, salvation. We'd been stricken and transfixed. We bathed in a world of sublime supreme love. "A love supreme," he bellowed. He repeated the phrase in every conceivable way, in every possible combination on his tenor saxophone and to our great surprise, the instrument became worn out, could no longer handle it. J.C. cast it aside and immediately found another medium. An enraptured voice, ecstatic, monotone, resuming indefatigably over and over again the same phrase as if for the musician the words of the Bhagavad Gita had become realized: "See now in this My body, the whole universe centered in one, including the moving and the unmoving." We were completely worn out, our hearts torn open, laid bare by this kind of sonic razor. J.C. had fallen completely silent. I was panting and blowing. Muriel, short of breath, was in tears, huge tears. Gleaming and crystalline tears rolling down her cheeks. But at the same time she was smiling. As for Nancy, her face was totally expressionless, only her eyes appeared opened onto a world that was invisible to us. It never crossed our minds to applaud. The silence lasted for quite some time . . . then all of a sudden we heard a deep laugh that started with an alto saxophone bass note, rose to a crescendo, slowly faded in a cascade of high notes and then died in a sharp snapping sound. Splivie, I'd forgotten all about Splivie! He was intoxicated, intoxicated from music and joy. This was the signal, and everyone broke into applause and conversation. The dazed barman snapped back into action and rushed over to his customer. A happy hubbub and miscellaneous noises. J.C bowed once more to the applause, and then left the stage.

There is a saying according to which nothing succeeds like success. We had the greatest difficulty approaching him on that night because everyone wanted a piece of him, to exchange a few words, even to get his autograph. But J.C. hadn't forgotten us, and he recognized us immediately. He kind of thought of us as old friends, those who hadn't waited for success to embrace him. It was with us he chose to hang out on that evening.

He wasn't the same J.C. we'd known. He was beaming, he was happy. Not with that joy that makes you want to shout from the rooftops, sing in the rain, or whatever else one does, but more that internal joy that burns like a fire—I was going to say that consumed him—and that made his face translucent. We settled in a bar I knew in Manhattan's Lower East Side, not far from Slug's, another jazz bar we often went to. I introduced him to the girls, and he really liked them.

"J.C., what you played tonight was a masterpiece. I'm serious when I say that, it's the best thing I've ever heard you play. You've found what you were looking for, haven't you?," I asked, happy.

He smiled.

"Yes, and perhaps also because I finally understood."

The waiter came over and interrupted us. J.C. only wanted a fruit juice. I was a little taken aback, since I remembered how much alcohol he'd drank on that night not that long ago at my place. We talked about music, and happiness. We congratulated him over and over again. He was of course delighted, but a little uncomfortable with all this praise.

Muriel, who up until then had just been listening, asked him, "You said a while back that you had found what you were looking for because you'd finally understood. What did you mean?"

"Your music was as beautiful as Muriel tonight," I said to tease her a little.

She poked her tongue out at me and turned to J.C., who was already answering her question.

"If I decided to not play for six months, it was to give me time to reflect on my art, on my failure. Not just with regard to audiences, but also my own failure, because I was not satisfied with what I was doing. So I spent a lot of time thinking, listening, and I also read a lot as well."

"But what was it you finally understood?," Muriel persisted.

"That there was too great a distance between my music and myself! Let me give you an example. There's this oriental fable that put me on the right track. A Sufi dervish tells the story. One day, a man went over to his beloved's home and knocked on the door. A voice answered: 'Who's there?' He answered, 'It's me.' The voice continued, 'There's not enough room here for you and for me.' The door remained shut and he walked away disappointed because his beloved had refused to see him. After living a year in solitude, hardship, and deep in thought, the man returned to his beloved's home. He knocked again. 'Who's there?,' a voice inquired. 'It's you,' he answered. She opened the door immediately."

We listened attentively to the story. It reminded me a little of those parables and proverbs the elders told back in the village.

"But what are you going to do, now that you've found what you were looking for?," Nancy asked him.

"Oh, that's not what I said, I've yet to find what I'm looking for. Will I ever find it? I might just have a better idea than I did before of where to look. That's already something. That's why I'm so happy tonight. I'd like to be so close to my music, so close that we would become one, that's the closest thing to godliness. And to die with it, preferably on stage, right at the very moment when I feel it as I did tonight."

He was silent for a while, and then with his usual modesty, added, "In any case, I wouldn't be the first to die on stage, now would I?"

We continued our conversation and drank until the bar closed.

I saw J.C. again once more, but I had no idea that would be the last time. Ah! If only I'd known! Is life only bearable when we don't know what lies ahead? Anyway, let's get back to that final meeting. But first, it's important to understand what J.C. and music meant to me and my friends in those days. Jazz was the thing, the place, the galaxy around which we organized our lives, and in the heart of that galaxy stood, like the sun, J.C. On Saturday evenings, penniless and with no means, we offered our services right around ten o'clock to a few restaurants that could use a helping hand when the rush of customers pouring out of the shows and movie theaters forced the owners to supplement the dishwashers, who couldn't keep up with the flow of customers. As soon as were paid, we started what in our jargon was known as "barhopping," doing the rounds of the local bistros to pick up here and there our friends who were each waiting for us in their favorite hangouts. And then, nocturnal birds that we were, our heads filled with lights and dreams, with or without the girls, we dove into the sonorous and initiatory darkness of New York's jazz clubs until the bright light of sunrise chased us out. Later, when we became political militants and supporters of the Black Panthers, this music took on a new meaning for us, becoming the artistic avant-garde of our struggle. Today, I'm the first to recognize that we took a little advantage of J.C. against his will, pulling the cover slightly over to our side, conferring on his marvelous music a political dimension. We'd even nicknamed him the Malcolm X of jazz. But this didn't really seem to bother him, and he'd never objected to the excessive use we made of him. Or maybe, even if he was more lucid than we were, he knew that music was intrinsically pure in the way that one can say that crystal is, and that our political adventures had ultimately no artistic consequence and did nothing to alter its very essence? Ah! J.C., you were more sincere than we were, your faith was of the disinterested kind. Could we truly say ours was? What was it we were really trying to say during those turbulent '60s when we talked about the liberation of Blacks and called for the end of exploitation of man by man? These words and bombastic principles used and then tossed in the face of the world—did they ever have any genuine concrete meaning? But you, when you told us that your music was a source of life, a means of elevating men to greater heights so that they might achieve what they really wanted in life, those weren't just empty words. And what evidence do I have? Well, you who'd once drank so much, you who'd tried just about every drug available, had all the women you desired, well, your music made it possible for you to give them all up. Your music was enough for you, perhaps too much even because you were becoming slightly ascetic, mystical even as when you talked about that trip you'd wanted to take to Africa, back to the Source. Did you have some kind of incline that Art would not be able to replace a real political and social revolution? That contrary to politics, which depends on manipulating crowds, salvation through Art is very much a personal matter, sort of like how one comes into this world alone and leaves it alone? In any case, you never tried to impose your ideas onto others as we had. But, J.C., in spite of yourself, in spite of the fact that we co-opted you, your music helped us, it helped our people because thanks to your music our people gained a new sensibility—it helped us uncover a new awareness and understanding of the world that had been burgeoning inside us. You could not have known how deeply moved we were by that masterpiece of yours, "Alabama," which lasted just two minutes and twenty seconds, and that you'd written in honor of those four black girls killed by a bomb that exploded in a church in Birmingham! Ah, J.C., those two minutes and twenty seconds of contained anger and sadness that somehow gave way to hope, springing forth from the depths of your sorrow that had come home triumphant in those high notes from your tenor saxophone that rose up into the skies above! During the '60s, I watched the closest companions of my generation sacrificed, massacred for the beliefs they held: believe me, J.C., your music upheld their faith. That's the artist's triumph over political militants, neither trying to persuade nor to bring happiness, at times even against their will. The artist allows each individual the pleasure of self-discovery as well as the discovery of those marvelous and extraordinary things that must exist somewhere out there in the universe . . .

Our last meeting? No, I won't say anything about it, it's just too sad. A J.C despondent, penniless, who'd been evicted from his apartment. Riots, Splivie's brother murdered. No, really, I don't see the point of talking about it.

5

J.C. was dead. We sat around listening to the recordings we had of his work. The volcanic love, the cataclysmic love one might even say, that came out of that instrument in the hands of that incredible musician was even more apparent. Nancy got up and turned on the radio to catch the evening news. Of course, the report had to do with J.C.'s passing. A lackluster, all-purpose obituary pretty much in the way they always are when it comes to famous people. They talked about the great musician, his wonderful concerts, that he stood among the best, etc., etc. But they didn't mention the J.C. we'd known, that desperate man, rejected by audiences and record labels, who dragged his carcass through the streets of New York while trying to nourish this music that incubated inside him. The J.C. who had been so happy when he thought he'd found the way, his way. Or the dejected man, evicted by the caretaker and struggling to find a new place to live between two riots . . . "We end our homage to this giant of jazz by playing one of the new tracks from the album he finished recording this past February and that unfortunately will only be released posthumously . . ."

I was shocked. A record I hadn't heard of! I didn't have enough time to turn on my recorder. As for Nancy, she was already glued to the tuner. We listened together. O heavens! J.C.! This was his unique way of stepping out of the chorus, slowly at first, then rising, surging, then eventually reining in the rhythmic section, but it was also a brand new J.C. Rather than escaping into the universe in an exclamation of joy, a scorching exhalation, this music was instead serene. It no longer had that stupendous celerity, that same vigor we'd known in him. J.C. seemed to be going in the opposite direction, descending further and further into the depths of his being, yet without completely masking those forces that were the unmistakable hallmarks of his music. One couldn't help feeling in the presence of a man disappointed in what he'd found—or perhaps even had failed to find. He seemed to have extracted all one could possibly get out of a tenor saxophone; and in some ways we weren't surprised to hear him at the end of the track trying his hand for the first time at the flute.

This was J.C.'s final message, a profound expression of what he was feeling during what were to be the last months of his life.

All of a sudden, I had the urge to write something. I grabbed hold of a sheet of paper and started scribbling.

When the time comes

and then that was it. I had to come up with something else, to write down a few words for me to remember this day with. Unfortunately, nothing came to me. The phone rang. It was Ornette Coleman, letting me know that J.C.'s casket would be at St. Peter's Church at the corner of 54th Street and Lexington Avenue, and asking me to get all my musician buddies to come along. On another note, he'd just learned that Ravi Shankar was in San Francisco and was trying to get in touch with him to see if he could make the trip. He also asked me call to check whether the poet Ted Joans was back from Paris. He ended by letting me know the funeral ceremony would take the form of a jazz concert, a jazz session of sorts. What a great idea! When I die, I'd like someone to play some live jazz music and, if that's not possible, then for someone to be kind enough to play "A Love Supreme" at the wake. I returned to my sheet of paper. Why did I so desperately want to write something? Was it in order to give this death some kind of meaning? But it was pointless trying to find some kind of greater meaning to death. J.C. always said that life had meaning, but not death. Had he found it? To be born, eat, grow up, make love, fight, search . . . and then die! J.C. was dead, he who had been so close to perfection, he who had glimpsed, in the space of a note, a sonority, the absolute that he'd tracked down perhaps in vain in the Bhagavad Gita! What was the meaning behind all of this? Perhaps in the end we really did overcomplicate things. And what if the meaning of life was life itself, and that the most important thing was to just live it? These and other thoughts raced through my mind. I was suffocating! I ran cold water over my neck for a while and then dried off. Nancy was still prostate in her chair. A calmness came over me. I picked up the sheet of paper I'd started writing on and wrote out these words:

When the time comes,
may he rise again in the glory
of his luminous sounds
to be the teacher of us all
and let his supreme vibrations show the way
to us,
the living,
and may his people for whom he sang
rise up with him . . .

No, I crossed out the last two lines "and may his people for whom, etc." I couldn't write that—I couldn't write that. I'd already cheated so much with the word "people," I'd already cheated so much with J.C and myself. There was only one thing I could be sure of: a man who could transport you toward distant stars with just one note, have you discover all those marvelous things both in this world and beyond, could not die. No, a man like J.C. could not die. I left my sheet of paper on the table, gathered all the records scattered all over the place, put them away carefully, and opened all the windows. I gave Nancy a kiss, opened the door, and walked out into the street. For a second I was dazed, not by the sun, but rather by the blinding glare from the windshield of a police car driving ahead of an ambulance. On the opposite side of the street, a young twelve-year-old black boy had just been killed by a white police officer, who was claiming before a hostile crowd of black bystanders that he'd acted in self-defense.

EMMANUEL DONGALA was born in 1941 in the Congo (Brazaville), a former French colony that achieved independence in 1960, a historical moment that coincided with his radical decision to come to study in the United States in the early 1960s—in those days, most francophone sub-Saharans chose further education in France. A chemistry professor at the University Marien Ngouabi in Brazzaville, he was forced to flee the Congo during civil conflict in the late 1990s. Through intervention from members of the U.S. State Department and that of a number of U.S. intellectuals and politicians, Dongala came with his family to the United States and was offered a professorship at Simon's Rock College of Bard in Great Barrington, Massachusetts. He is widely considered one of the most important living African writers. Novels include *Un fusil dans la main, un poème dans la poche* (1974, Grand Prix Ladislas Dormandi); *Le Feu des origines* (1987), for which he was awarded the Grand Prix Littéraire d'Afrique noire and the Charles Oulmont Prize (published in English as *The Fire of Origins*); *Les petits garçons naissent aussi des étoiles* (1998; published in English as *Little Boys Come from the Stars*); *Johnny chien méchant* (2002, Cezam Prix Littéraire Inter CE; published in English as *Johnny Mad Dog* and adapted for the cinema as Johnny Mad Dog); and *Photo de groupe au bord du fleuve* (2010).

DOMINIC THOMAS is the Madeleine L. Letessier Professor of French and Francophone Studies at the University of California, Los Angeles. His books include *Nation-Building, Propaganda, and Literature in Francophone Africa* (IUP, 2002), *Black France: Colonialism, Immigration, and Transnationalism* (IUP, 2007), and *Africa and France: Postcolonial Cultures, Migration, and Racism* (IUP, 2013).

Lightning Source UK Ltd.
Milton Keynes UK
UKHW041255020221
377887UK00013B/530